DOUBLE DIPPIN'

NICOLE FáLon GARRETT

Send inquiries to P.O. Box 45892, Los Angeles, CA 90045

Printed in the United States of America
Second Printing.

ISBN Agency:
978-0-9818608-0-0

Author photo by Ancel S. Hall
www.ashphotoagency.com
Cover photo by Siri Stafford, Getty Images
Copy Editors: Carolyn Patricia Scott and Van To
Content Editors: William A. Golden and Sharon Renfroe

Disclaimer

This book is a work of fiction and is not based on actual events.
Characters, names, events and locations are based on the author's
creativity or used solely for fictitious purposes.

www.doubledippin2.com

No painter's brush, nor poet's pen
In justice to her fame
Has ever reached half high enough
To write a mother's name.

~Author Unknown

This book is dedicated to all the Mothers who have influenced me in life.

My mother and inspiration for all I do, Delores.
My grandmothers, Birdie and Elizabeth.
My aunts: Aunt Lue, Doris, Bernice, Margaret, Liz, Ivory, Annette, Joanne, Charlotte, Deidre, Karen, Versie, and Twyla.
And all my cousins: Margarita, Deborah Ann, Doris, Lynette, Dolly, Lois, Henrietta, Crystal, Vanessa, LaTrece, LaTonya, and Angel.

Observation of your actions and measurement of your words have guided me on more occasions than you'll ever know. Thank you all for your snow angels in the blistery storms in Chicago and your footprints in the sand on the sunny beaches in Montego Bay. I would say, "I love you all very very much," but that's a tad bit too mushy. LMAO

Prologue

Bulbs flash, artists sketch, and columnists scribble in notepads. All in an attempt to document what has been coined "the murder trial of the decade."

Inmate 30.000.000 is the identification tag granted to my friend in the newspapers, on television, and by bloggers. A noble deed if it can increase ratings, circulation, or website hits.

Chicago's 30 millionth accused felon is being exploited during this election year by both sides. Mayor Daley's platform is arguing that the city is tough on criminals. His opponent claiming that this is proof of the administration's leniency on crime, misappropriation of city funds, and the need for more police officers.

Today, the courtroom seems darker than usual and, although it is typical Windy City cold outside, the air is thick and unforgiving in here. I look up front for my regular seat.

PROLOGUE

The jury has been sequestered for three months and in deliberation for four days. When they told the judge that they were hung and could not agree, he sent them back. Now they've made their decision.

I watch my best friend being escorted into the courtroom. The guards, both about 6'4" and 600 pounds combined, tower over the subdued figure who they practically drag into the over-crowded limited space. Shackled hands and feet slow the pace of my once vibrant friend, partner, and confidant. A common criminal is what they want us to believe. But that's not so.

The orange jumpsuit appears worn from too many years of use and hangs off the undernourished body of the media-made criminal. Unkempt hair covers the lifeless eyes and protruding jaws of a once full face, void. Absent, the smile that used to shake the foundation of any gathering. Missing, the gait that cleared the path upon entrance. Gone, the love for life, the desire to live, the will to go on.

Our eyes meet and I can tell that in that instant, we both go back to where it all began.

Overkill

will define herself. naturally. will
talk/walk/live/& love her images.
her beauty will be.
—Haki Madhubuti

*Amber*____
October 2005

The hand-written instructions are clear and simple.
Objective: *One assailant. Bedroom, first door on the right.
Bring him out alive.*

My ski mask and night goggles are snuggly in place before I
take my Glock 9 mm out of my hip holster. The leather gloves keep
the 80 watt from burning my fingertips while I kill the outside
light. Slowly cracking the door to the house and peeking around
reveals that no one's lurking in the shadows.

Quietly stepping inside and quickly squatting with my back
against the wall positions me to thoroughly scan the family room,

dining room, and kitchen. Convinced the coast is clear, I stand and tiptoe on cat's feet to the first room on the right.

The door is ajar and the TV suddenly goes off. The crack in the door isn't wide enough to allow enough visibility for a spot sur-veillance; however, a drawer on the left side of the room can be heard sliding slowly on its rails.

I quickly push the door, drop to the floor and aim the gun in the direction of the moving drawer. The assailant is standing there with a gun already pointed at my head. Rolling just in time to miss being shot, I pull my trigger.

Suddenly, an armed man pops out of the closet. At the same time, another one appears in front of the bathroom door. "Oh, shoot!"

There was only supposed to be one, I think as I dash behind the bed for shield. After they've shot their first rounds at me and are reloading, I stand and blast the two of them.

The lights flick on. The marquis above all three life-size props, each with two bullet holes to the head, flashes the words MORTALLY WOUNDED.

"Amber, you were supposed to shoot them in the shoulder," he yells as he does everyday that I make it to this stage of the practice.

I lift my gun and fire three times, shooting each prop in the shoulder.

"Done," I smirk at the new status report on the marquis which now flashes POST-MORTEM SHOULDER WOUND.

Exhausted and exhilarated, I walk towards the door to leave the simulation suite. My headache, earache, and toothache are coming in loudly clapping and laughing.

"Well, well, well, if it ain't the Black Widow Spider seeping her poison onto everyone in her path again. That's what you call *overkill.*" The contemporary equivalent of the Three Stoogers blocks the exit.

"Well, well, well, if it isn't Moe, Larry, and Curly believing that personality is a character trait afforded to the beauties, but not for the geeks," I motion my hand at them, "who believe that being annoying and obnoxious will suffice."

Attempting to politely go around them becomes obviously futile when Moe reaches out and touches my stomach, forcing me to pull out the bulldozer. I grab Moe's wrist and twist his arm, flipping him on his back before bringing both my elbows up and driving them down with force on Larry and Curly's shoulders. They fall to their knees as I step back and put my foot on Moe's neck.

"Don't ever put your fucking hands on me again. Got it?" I look down on him and twist my foot on his neck before removing it.

Curly, who's still on the floor holding his shoulder, looks up at me in pain, "But we didn't touch you. So what was that for?"

"Just don't like you. That's all." I step around them to leave the simulation suite and head up to my room to shower. They continue to be idiots in my absence.

"Man, what size you think her waistline is?"

"No bigger than a twenty-four, I bet."

"I'm telling you, looking up at her with that five inch stiletto on my neck was turning me on."

"Hell yeah. She can put her foot on my neck any day."

They all laugh.

Wuttin' My Fault

Art, like morality, consist in drawing the line somewhere.

—G. K. Chesterton

Chase _____

"So what *chu* gon' do 'bout it?"

"What I'm gon' do? I'll tell you what I'ma do. I'ma whup yo' punk ass!" And before I know it, I have Malik by the neck with one hand and the back of his pants with the other hand, and then I toss his frail frame across the room. He lands on the plastic-covered cream couch, flips over, and crashes down on the cocktail table, splattering it and sending shards of glass flying in all directions.

My mother instinctively jumps up to protect her trifling, crack head baby boy. "Chay Chay, why'd you have to go and do that?" She rushes toward Malik who is losing blood from somewhere, but I'm faster.

I get that neck again and pimp-slap him while he unsuccess-fully puts his hands up to protect his face. *I guess no one told him that his pretty boy days are long gone.*

Pulling him by his matted, wooly mane, I drag my baby brother to his basement room—making sure he hits every stair on the way down. The dingy basement feels moist and smells like a mixture of the orangutan cage and the chicken coop at Brookfield Zoo.

He struggles to break loose before I throw him head first into his closet. He's no match for me. Both of us were on our high school football team, but I was the All-American quarterback in high school and college. Not to mention that I practice martial arts and work out at least five days a week as if I'm still an All-Star athlete. And at six feet tall, I have a couple inches on him in height.

Voice trembling and frantic, my mother is yelling at me in the background, "Chase Amanuel Livingston, you stop it right now!"

Any other time, my mother calling me by my birth name would have stopped me dead in my tracks, but not today. He's messed up big time. One of my boys from the neighborhood called to tell me that while Malik was on one of his delusional rampages where he thinks "the aliens are coming" or some other crazy shit, he fired off twelve rounds in the house.

Twelve rounds?! That means that he had to reload the 38-caliber that he was using. So, no type of mind adjustment kicked in between the time he shot the first six and the time he had to go back to the basement for the second clip. *Naw, he has gotta go,* I think.

5

"Pack yo' shit!"

He glances at me and then surveys the three possible exits trying to figure out an escape path.

"NOW!" I yell.

Malik looks defeated. This was my room for ten years before it was his. The terrain is as familiar to me as it is to him. He doesn't have a chance.

"Man, Chay Chay, why you extra'd out on me? I said I was sorry. It ain't gon' happen no mo'."

You damn right it ain't gon' happen no mo', I think as I pick up the broom that is propped against the stairs. "That's the same thing you said when you took off in Mrs. Taylor's car when she sent you to get her some Harold's Chicken cuz her sugar was acting up."

He looks down at his feet that only has a shoe on the left foot—don't know when he lost the other one.

"And remember when the post office fired you for suspected mail tampering? First real job you ever had. You woulda done federal time if they had one *ounce* of proof."

"Now that wuttin' my fault. Po' Boy said he done that fa' six years and it always went smooth. The gov'ment just gave dem people another check."

I ignore his explanation of events, although he ain't never admitted to having any involvement in the scam up 'til this point.

"And what about the case of the feet-having jewelry box that all of our family heirlooms was in? Stuff from Grandma and Big Momma."

"But Chay Chay....."

"But my *ass*! And did you forget that you were too high to make it to Grandpa's funeral?"

I walk towards Malik with the broom and he scrambles to stuff some dirty, soiled clothes into a black garbage bag. Before he's completely done, I snatch him by his arm and lead him out the back basement door to the alley where my car is parked. I push him into the backseat.

"Where we going, Chay Chay?"

"To hell if we don't pray." I slam the car door and walk around to the other side to get in while Malik naturally scrambles to get out. The child-proof locks are engaged because I knew his crack head mind would be plotting. He tries to let down the electric windows and the car isn't even turned on yet.

Crack kills. And it burns away brain cells before you're dead.

I see my mother looking out the window crying. I don't know if she's crying because I *hurt* the crack head or because he *is* a crack head. I start the car. Malik pushes the power window so that he can open the door from the outside. Of course, they're locked. *I guess he thinks I'm on crack too.* I pull off. As I exit the alley, I see two squad cars turn onto my mother's block.

Three hours later, I watch my brother board a plane from Midway to LAX where my Uncle Steve will be waiting for him. I look at my watch and hurry to my car to attempt to beat rush hour. Jazz is waiting. Can't wait to see my baby.

Riff Raff
& In-Laws

Love is the irresistible desire
to be irresistibly desired.

—Robert Frost

Asia____

We peel our sweaty bodies apart. *"Ssshhhhit!"* is coming out of my mouth at the same time that *"Gaahdamn!"* is coming out of his.

"Shaun, that was absolutely incredible." I run my fingers across my husband's dark curly mane that has been moistened over the last three hours and kiss his full luscious lips.

"Yeah, I know," is all he is able to whisper in his labored breath.

I consider doing the "one thing" that I know will get him ready for another three hours, but he had just gotten back from Sudan three hours and ten minutes ago. I jumped him at the threshold. And, with the eight hour difference, he is exhausted.

I wipe his forehead and chest with the Hugo Boss handkerchief that is on the nightstand and then watch him slip into a deep sleep.

Damn you're gorgeous, I think then drift off into dreams and ringing. *The phone?* I quickly pick up the receiver.

"Asia speaking." The dial tone buzzes in my ear from our home phone while another phone keeps ringing in the distance. I look around the room until I locate Shaun's cell phone. I ignore it, close my eyes, and attempt to go back to sleep. Two minutes later, the phone rings again. I reluctantly pull myself out of bed, walk over to the armoire, and pick up his cell phone to turn it off. As I'm about to hold down the power button, I notice that the caller id says private.

Who would call twice from a blocked number? I wonder. "Hello?" I say more as a question than a greeting.

"Uh, yeah, hello. Is, uh, Jamal there?"

"Sorry Dear, you must have the wrong number," I say to the woman who pauses as if checking the number that she'd dialed.

"Uh, yeah, I guess I do." She hangs up abruptly.

Interrupt my after sex nap and she couldn't even say 'I'm sorry.' *Rude.*

I shower, put on my clothes, and head down to our home library to finish the business for the party. I shuffle through the papers once more—being careful to put everything back in its proper place. All of the documentation is color-coded. The yellow is here—red, orange, green, pink. The lavender is missing.

I sort through the neatly stacked piles of quotes, names, dates, and timelines. *Lavender, lavender?* I glance from my desk over to the conference table, but the high-back, leather office chairs are in the way.

The intercom snaps me out of search mode, "Mrs. Duvall, you have a visitor," Ida announces.

I push the intercom button, "Ida, how long have you been my housekeeper?"

"Um, about, I say, seven years or so."

"Well, do you think that 'um about say seven years or so' is long enough to understand that when I *specifically* ask *not* to be disturbed that's what I mean?"

"Yes Ma'am, Senora Duvall. I'm sor—"

"Don't be sorry, be obedient. Send them away! Whoever it is."

"Uhh, Miss, excuse me Miss. You can't go in that way," Ida drops the receiver of the intercom phone system that I had installed to screen out the riff raff and in-laws. The double doors to my library are flung opened with force.

Amber strides in wearing a full-length, camel-colored cashmere coat with fox tuxedo. She unties the belt of her coat, turns to Ida who is hot on her heels, and says, "Ida, your name *is* Ida, right?"

Ida nods.

"Ida, I need you to hang my coat in the guest closet and not on the coat rack by the door for obvious reasons."

Amber removes her fox cuff hat and her bouncy curls fall below her shoulders. She tosses the hat on top of the coat in Ida's arms. "And close the door behind you," she instructs with the flick of her hand.

Who the hell does she think she is?

Ida looks at me for confirmation and, after I give her the nod, she turns to leave. Before Ida closes the door Amber says, "Oh, one more thing, Ida. Hold all calls and visitors because Mrs. Duvall is incredibly busy right now."

Amber twirls on her heels and makes a beeline straight to my desk, making certain her eel skin Casadei boots announce her determination with every step.

"Amber, who gave you access to the penthouse? No one can get up here without proper keys and authorization." I try not to allow my disgust to seep out, to no avail.

"And hello to you too, Mrs. Duvall. Me? I'm doing fine. Thanks for asking." Her sarcasm makes my ears ring.

I push away from my desk and pull out the bottom drawer in search of the missing documents. "What do you want now, Amber? Our monthly meeting is not until next week."

"Meeting? Oh, is that the term for it this week?" Amber slides onto the chaise lounge and crosses her legs as if she plans to stay a while. "Why don't you just call it what it is? A payoff, a bribe, a little bit of hush money." She smiles, obviously ready for combat.

Looking at Amber, everything about her says sugar-sweet. Her smile whispers come hither and the brightness of her penetrating black eyes is practically paralyzing. Smooth, flawless light-brown skin with a hint of red makes her appear to have a constant glow.

Sugar-sweet my ass.

"I asked you a question and I need an answer," I cut my eyes at her from behind my desk. "If you want to amuse yourself with the guessing game, you need to find another playmate because I don't partake in those games anymore."

The smile falls from her face and her eyes become cold and distant.

"Well, in that case, I'll get straight to the point." She moves her hair behind her ears revealing the round opaque ruby that matches the three stone necklace that she's wearing. "I need my uh, what can we call it…….package. Yeah, I need my package early this month because I hear there's a huge event this weekend and I need to—"

I raise my hand for her to shut up. "Fine."

My checkbook is already on the desk. I reach into the secret pocket on the side and pull out the money order for $2,000. I quickly write her name, saying each syllable, "Am…ber Cher….ring….ton." I pass it to her. "Is there anything else before you leave?"

Her glare makes the temperature in the library drop even more. "Yeah, there is as a matter of fact." She stands showing her statuesque frame. "I want to sit at the head table."

"The head table is full."

"Well, I'm sure you'll figure something out, Mrs. Duvall. You always do," she snaps as she walks around the chaise and storms toward the door, leaving as quickly as she had entered. I exhale a sigh of relief at her departure.

Ugh. What is wrong with that girl?

Turning in my chair, I admire what hard work and dedication has afforded me and what Amber evidently wants to destroy. Our home library is spectacular. I love to see the look of amazement in visitors' eyes when they see what I've done with the place. I twirl my colorless, five-carat, princess-cut wedding ring around my finger as I remember the first time I gave a tea party.

"Oh, my God. Asia, this is beautiful," said Mrs. McClendon, the police chief's wife. Where ever did you find an authentic *Venus de Milo*?

"France. Where else?" I giggle. "I went to an exhibit at a widow's home and I absolutely would not leave without them, no matter what the price." I waved my hand around to direct her attention to the other three podiums that held encased sculptures of Justitia as *Lady Justice,* Rodin's *The Thinker,* and Michelangelo's *Statue of David.*

Mrs. McClendon asked the same question that many before her had asked, "Are you willing to sell any of these?"

Yes, our library is spectacular. At last count, there were 5800 books. Guests enter through stained-glass French doors. Bacci Truscelli, the world famous Italian painter, designed a montage of colonial history on our high ceiling in an array of colors.

Each wall of the octagon-shaped library is donned with famous paintings by well known artists. Except for the wall with me on it, of course. Couldn't have a library without that, now could we? It's actually a painting of my prom queen picture. High cheekbones, big sunshine eyes, luxurious lashes and a runway smile is a masterpiece within itself. *Hmm. That's the best painting in the place.*

Now where was I? I walk to the conference table and search the paperwork. The marble floor creates excellent sound effects under my Cole Haan's.

Where are the lavender sheets? The winery bids are on the lavender paper and need to be arranged so that confirmation can be sent out to finalize the order for the highest bidder. The party is less than a week away and we have to allow sufficient time for delivery.

When the word got out about Shaun's 40th birthday party, I was contacted by PR reps from five local wineries asking if they could donate the wine. *Hey, the richer you are, the more free stuff you get. It's the American way.* You know, like teachers get summer breaks, lawyers get their speeding tickets thrown out, and police get to commit crimes. Being offered free things go with the territory of being wealthy. That's just one of the perks.

Okay, this is ridiculous. I walk back to my desk and as I reach over to page Ida, the phone rings. "Yes, Mrs. Duvall speaking."

"*Oooh,* Mrs. Duvall, huh? Sounds pretty professional for a high-society bum."

"It's *called* having old money, Jazz. Get you some and learn the lingo." We laugh. "And stop messing with me. I'm about ready to pull my hair out getting ready for this party on Saturday."

"Even the tracks glued in the back that your husband doesn't know about?" Jazz jokes.

"Ha, ha, real funny."

We've had a going joke since we met at Jazz's wedding where Shaun was Chase's best man. My hair is thick and hangs pass the middle of my back. One of Chase's ghetto cousins wanted to know, "Did chu use super grow on yo' hair o' is dat a weave?" And she just stuck her hand in the back of my head and yanked really hard, before saying, "*Daaammmn!* That's yo' shit. You must got some Indian in yo' blood."

"I need a drink," I plop back down in my chair.

"It's eleven in the morning, Asia," Jazz says. "Only a certain breed of monkeys drinks before five."

"Well smack my ass and call me Curious George." I push the intercom button, "Double-shot Ida." I release the button, "And if you know like I do, you'll invest in a flask before those stiff necks at the courthouse drive you crazy. Just like this party is driving me crazy."

"Speaking of the party, I'm faxing you three appellate court judges and the deputy mayor's info so that you can add them to the VIP list. My phone has been ringing off the hook today about *your* little soirée."

"Trust me when I say, nothing that I do is *ever* little. Fifteen hundred people have already RSVP'd on this side of the globe, not to mention Shaun's international connections. So, Jazz, don't hate the playa."

"Well, play on, playa. My secretary is faxing that stuff right now. Oh, and by the way, I made our spa appointments at Mario Tricoci for Thursday."

"Thanks, Jazzy. What would I do without you?"

"I'm sure you'd think of something being the expert party-planner that you are. Now, I gotta go. Some of us have real jobs. Oh yeah, and stop wasting colored paper on stupid stuff 'cuz I know you've pulled it out. *Please* spare the trees. Later, playa."

After we hang up, I decide to check on Shaun. As I approach the bedroom, I hear him talking. It sounds like he's in a heated discussion.

"Which language do I need to say 'no' in before you get it?" he's saying as I enter the room. When he sees me, he immediately hangs up the phone and turns it off.

I go over to the bed and kiss him. "Who was that?"

"Nobody. Just an upset client who called me about a deal that went bad." Shaun has this bad twitching eyebrow lately. He rubs his eye, jumps up, and goes to the bathroom.

I pick up his cell phone and turn it back on to check the call log to make sure I remove that client from the party list, but the last call was the one that I answered over two hours ago. *I thought he said that the client had called him. I guess I was wrong.*

I check the outgoing calls. *Hmm. That's weird.* Shaun had called someone stored simply as LS. Well, in his line of business, it's important to keep identities as classified as possible. I turn his cell phone back off and take off my clothes so that I can join him in the shower. I'm ready for another three hours. Hope he is.

Double Wrap

A man is only as faithful as his options.

—Chris Rock

Chase ____

This bowtie has gotta go, I think, slipping it off with my left hand and stuffing it in the seat cushion. *Hopefully, Jazzy doesn't notice.*

As we ride along Lakeshore Drive, I look out at Lake Michigan and try to forget about the fight I had with my brother earlier this week, although my knuckles are still sore. I'm amazed by the lake's calmness this late in the fall. Usually its temperament has changed by the end of September. Maybe this is a sign of a mild winter.

The yachts and boats are still out in large numbers, and people stroll on the beaches unaffected by the harsh elements that usually have left the shoreline barren by now. Many of the trees still have leaves on them. There is tranquility in the air—serene, still, unruffled. Kinda eerie actually.

As we pull up to Chicago's Shedd Aquarium, the largest indoor aquarium in the world, there are lines of limousines parked along the curb. Our driver pulls into the space that another limo has just left. He comes around and opens my door.

I hop out and extend my hand for Jazz. When her clear, open toe sandal touches the pavement, her split shifts to expose a perfectly smooth, bronze thigh. Her violet velvet dress embraces every curvaceous dip and makes me wish I could be either violet or velvet tonight. I smile into her hazel eyes causing Jazz to reveal her deep dimples. She loops her arm through mine, sending electric shock waves through my body.

As we walk the red carpet to the entrance of the building, I notice how many men are staring at my baby. I know why. Jazzy's walk is musical. Whatever motion she makes is inviting—even hypnotizing. She has the grace of any goddess and is as sleek as a Black Panther. I lift her chin and gently kiss her lips. *Mine, mine,* I think as I see a few of her admirers look away, obviously not wanting to see me fondle the object of their night's wet dream.

We enter the foyer of the aquarium. The party doesn't officially start for another half hour, but it already looks like the floor of the New York Stock Exchange. People are gathered around a number of fish tanks that line the walls.

We stop at the blotched, deep-red oceanic seahorses that have drawn a huge crowd. One man is preaching about how they will be extinct in another thousand years if humans don't stop catching them for love elixirs, key chains, and to find a cure for arthritis. "There's never gonna be a cure for arthritis," he says as people begin to disperse in flight from his tirade.

One woman rebuts under her breath, "Extinction is inevitable because the males are the ones who have to get pregnant and have the babies."

She has a good point. I saw the male seahorses giving birth on the Discovery Channel. The female shoots about 200 eggs into the male seahorse and he delivers in about twenty-one days, then they start over again.

Definitely a flaw in nature.

Finally, the doors to the main hall are opened and you can hear the band playing Luther's "Bad Boy." Shaun is a Luther Vandross fanatic. Upon entrance to the dining hall, one of about forty hostesses asks our name and escorts us to the head table.

We are greeted by Asia whose long red sleeveless dress with silver satin trim around the top of the halter matches the color scheme of the party. "Jasmine, Chase."

Jazz touches the material of Asia's dress. "Asia, is this the infamous stretch metal dress that you told me about?"

"Nicole Miller's one of a kind." Asia twirls around in a circle modeling before she gives Jazz that double-kiss thing that she likes to do when she's in her element.

"I like. I like." Jazz says.

Asia hugs me, pecks me on the cheek, and grabs Jazz's hand all in one motion. "Come Jazzy, there's someone who you absolutely have to meet." *Oh, here we go,* I think.

We walk pass a group of sixty-year old white women singing like Luther, "I know it's hard to resist. This is the party no one wanted to miss." *What y'all know 'bout that?*

While letting the distance increase between me and Jazz and Asia, I quickly scan the room to find Shaun. Unable to locate him, I use my full-proof radar—the women. I look at the women to see which direction they're pretending not to look towards. Bingo. Works every time. I spot him encircled by a group of old, white politicians.

As best friends in high school, girls used to call us salt and pepper because of our color contrast. Being half Puerto-Rican, Shaun is only a few shades darker than the men he's talking to. Or more accurately the men he's entertaining. Animation is definitely one of his better qualities. Just as I am walking up, Shaun says something that makes the group burst out into uncontrollable laughter.

"I guess the joke's on me, huh?" I ask.

"C-Dog, what's up man? You know everybody here. Who doesn't know Chase?"

Most of these men had one or more of my paintings in their homes. And lately they've been sending me more business than I can handle. I shake hands with all the men and make small talk before I say, "Oh, I almost forgot what I came over here for. Shaun your lovely wife requests your presence." On that note, we make our escape.

"Thanks for rescuing me from the pacemaker club." Shaun adjusts his cufflinks and straightens the already straight collar of his Zoot Suit Peak Lapel Tuxedo. "I think they were trying to initiate me by boring me to death." Since his strut is as exaggerated as George Jefferson's, when we start walking, his tuxedo jacket which is almost to his knees swings from side to side.

"How do I look?" he asks.

"Like shit."

"Good. 'Cuz if you hate it, the ladies gon' love it." He struts with even more confidence now. "Dog, guess who's here?" Shaun grins while adjusting his red tie.

Shit, everybody in Chicago's upper-echelon.

"Remember that chick that I knocked the bottom out of last month while her husband and my assistant were finalizing his million dollar purchase in the next room?"

"Yeah, what's her name again?"

"Miranda Bayard. I guess nobody told him about bringing sand to a business meeting. Now she's trying to hook up after the party."

"Where she at?" I scan the room.

"Can you say hot, hot, *hot* ass pink?" He's smiling that stupid ass smile again.

She's easy to spot in her pinker than pink crepe dress with *waaay* more cleavage than her dress wants to allow and a matching magenta mink shawl.

I frown. "Man, I wouldn't fuck her ass with a dildo. She looks nasty."

"That's what you say now. Look at those lips." He points across the room. "You see them luscious lips?" Shaun licks his lips then bites down on the bottom one.

"Yeah, I see them," I respond although I only see lips minus the lusciousness that has him squirming.

"Let her get those lips around yo' dick, then talk to me. *Mmm, mmm.* I'm telling you man, now I know what they *mean* by the jaws of death. She had me screaming Hail Mary's up in that bad boy." He laughs. I don't.

"Yeah right. Well, I hope you used a double wrap with her nasty ass. She looks like she could burn the skin off a dick quicker than a chemistry experiment."

Shaun laughs again. I raise my eyebrow while waiting for an answer.

"Hey, when I'm in a storm, I have on my raincoat, hat, and rubber boots—just in case I step *up in* some shit." Shaun's left brow twitches and I know he's lying.

"Damnit, Shaun! You ain't gon' be happy 'til yo' dick fall off. If not for yourself, at least think of Asia."

"Chase, lighten up, Dog. I'm just living the life I was blessed to live. I mean, you a halfway decent looking brotha. No where near as fine as me." He rubs his chin in compliment. "But, you can still come over to the other side. The side where the *real* men stand." He pokes his chest out, I guess, like a "real man" would. I want to cave it in. "Hey, and I understand that you scared. It can be intimidating. Only real men can juggle two and three women at a time."

"Real men, okay." I laugh. "Yo' married ass better grow the fuck up before it's too late."

"Yeah, I'll make sure I do that.....next year." He laughs.

A welcomed interruption from Congressman Riley with his bad breath and matching toupee comes just in time to save Shaun from the cursing out that he was about to get. Doesn't matter. He's heard it all before.

From that moment on, we never have time to finish our conversation. For the next two hours, we juggle and entertain the people on this side of the hall while our wives work the other side of the room.

The lights flash three times to signal that dinner would be served. The music retreats from 70's Motown to 19th Century Chopin. Everybody gradually walks to their tables.

As I pull the chair out for Jazz, I look around the table and am a little confused by the people who are chosen to sit at the head table. Of course, we're supposed to be there because I've been his best friend since high school. But none of these other people are close friends of Shaun's. Asia has Alderman Lipinski, the alderman of the ward that they live in at the table along with his wife. A local fashion designer, Barbara Bates and her husband. Sitting next to them is an extremely striking, young woman who Asia introduces as simply "Amber." And the last couple is Leo Bayard and his very pink wife, Miranda, who by some stroke of luck, just so happens to be seated next to Shaun.

Now, how the hell did that happen? I wonder.

"This is absolutely everything that I hoped it would be." Asia, like her husband, Shaun, doesn't wait for a response or confirmation from anyone. "Look at how many people came to the party." She throws her hair from side to side with each sentence. She's as animated as he is. Match made in heaven.

"Baby, I think you may have to turn forty again next year. What do you think?" Everyone at the table shares a chuckle.

"Yes, I can see that you are the master planner," Amber says more to herself than to Asia.

Asia is so busy praising herself for the "wonderful" job that she'd done preparing for the party and rambling on about some damn colored paper, that she doesn't notice her husband twitching in his seat. The twitch that I recognize as the "hand job under the table" twitch. Miranda's hand remains in Shaun's lap for most of dinner before he finally chokes—the "jack off successful" choke.

"Are you okay, Honey?" Asia pats Shaun on his back in an attempt to free up his windpipe. Little does she know, she is focusing on the wrong pipe.

"Perfect, Love. Everything's perfect. Thanks to you," Shaun says and kisses Asia softly on her cheek as the double meaning flies right pass her.

As if on cue, Amber reaches across the table for the coffee creamer and knocks Miranda's red wine off the table into Miranda's lap.

"Oh me, oh my. Did I do that? I can be so clumsy at times," Amber quickly parades around Leo and uses her handkerchief to wipe off Miranda's dress, but while in the process she spills the au jus onto Miranda's hot pink disaster as well.

Amber smacks her lips, "Gosh darn it, we're just gonna have to go to the ladies room to handle this." She practically lifts Miranda out of her seat and ushers her toward the restroom.

When they return, Miranda looks a little flustered as she tells her husband that they would have to leave.

"Oh no, don't go. You gon' make me feel bad," Amber cries melodramatically as she and Miranda exchange cat glares.

"No, no. Accidents happen," Miranda replies through clenched teeth. "I just need to treat this before the stain settles in." The couple shakes hands with Shaun and Asia before they leave the party. *Glad I didn't have to shake that hand.*

After we finish our dinner and sing Stevie Wonder's version of happy birthday, the rest of the party goes without incident. A little dancing, a little talking, and a whole lot of drinking.

I find Jazz sitting on a love seat in the lounge area. I plop down next to her and she rests her head on my shoulder. We compare notes about who's who and what's what as the guests begin to file out of the Shedd Aquarium.

She's straining to keep her eyes open, but manages to say, "Honey, make sure you remember to get that bowtie that you stuffed in the seat of the limo. I spent a lot of money on that thing."

I smile, kiss her forehead, and take my phone from my breast pocket to call the driver. We say our goodbyes to Asia and Shaun who don't look the least bit tired although it's 3 a.m.

"*Oooh.* Thanks for coming," Asia says as she saunters over to Jazz still bubbling over from the night's event. Double-kiss.

Shaun and I do the man dap and we all vow to make it to church in the morning. Shaun's left brow twitches.

Good Blood

It's easier to build strong children
than to repair broken men.

—Frederick Douglass

Teenage Girl, Louisiana ____

August 2000

"Damnit, Girl I know it don't take dat long. You den had dis man waiting fifteen minutes."

"Coming Daddy."

I quickly drop the last Losartan tablet on the counter and crush it with the spoon. I scrape the ground up pill into the capsule, then drop all twenty of the new capsules into the Vitamin B-12 bottle and put it back in the medicine cabinet.

I brush the front of my burgundy and gray, pleated Catholic school skirt and fold down my bobbie socks. I dab under my eyes to keep the tears from smearing my mascara and inhale deeply to settle the butterflies in my stomach.

This is about to be a long night.

"Let's go Trooper?" I say to my reflection in the mirror. When I step out of the bathroom, my daddy startles me. I jump. I don't know why I'm surprised because I can smell the liquor from his breath and his pores as soon as I open the door. He's leaning against the wall like it's his sole support. "Let me inspect you, Girl," he slurs and spits at me. He bends down on his knees, puts his nose up my skirt to my private spot, and sniffs like this would be the last breath that he ever takes, taking it deeply into his lungs. The scratchy bristles of his beard rub roughly against my inner thighs. Satisfied that I had freshened up sufficiently after the last guy, he stands, or more accurately stumbles, to his feet and walks away without saying another word. The tears begin rolling again. I hold my head back and wipe them away.

"Let's go Trooper."

In the front room, an overweight sixty-something year old man with a hairline that appears to be running from his face, is waiting patiently and anxiously with his belly protruding over his Lee jeans, which could have walked without his assistance—using either the thick dirt, the pissy smell, or the pole sticking straight out his zipper.

"Hi, I'm Sweet Cheeks. Come on back," I chime musically and invitingly.

"Wait, let me look at cha." He points a wrinkled finger that seems to be inflicted with an uncontrollable shake or a twitch, I couldn't tell which, and signals for me to turn around. "Mm, hmm. How old you be anyhow? Bet' not be over fourteen. I told Leroy I ain't want no old twat. I ain't paying a dime for nan twat over fourteen."

What the hell is a twat? "I'm thirteen and a half," I lie, bat my eyelashes, and put on my school girl smile. Only because I remember the last time I told one of the old farts that I was 16, he left. Daddy was so mad that he beat me until the police came. One of the neighbors felt sorry for me that day.

"I guess I can make do."

Old ass twitching fucker. "Good then let's get to it."

I lead Twitch to the red room. The 20-watt light bulb is just bright enough to see the red carpet and red sheets, which I notice were not changed after the last guy. Great. He walks up behind me and cups my peach-sized breast in his hands. He begins to grind on my ass.

"Say my name."

Is your name Ben or Gay because that's all I can sense right now?

Now he's panting real hard. He pushes me down on the bed so that he can get a better position on his grind and slobs on my ear-lobe.

"Say my name."

I muffle, "Go Trooper" incoherently into the pillow. *Just let this be over soon.*

"Louder. Say it louder. I can't hear you, Sweet Cheeks."

"Big Daddy. Work it Big Daddy. Oooh wee. That's just how I like it."

I start gyrating to rush the process along. As soon as I make one full motion, Twitch lets out a howl. His body jerks then stiffens before he collapses on my back. If it wasn't for the panting and the continual flow of saliva down my neck, I would have thought the man had croaked.

I push him off me, get out the bed, and dust myself off. I look in the mirror to fix my hair, but nothing is out of place.

"Where ya' think you'se going? We ain't done yet." Twitch pulls out his limp wet dick and says, "Come here, Sweet Cheeks."

I move slowly hoping with all my might that he's not wanting what I think he wants. By the time I make it to the bed, he has already taken his pants all the way off.

"Come closer, I'm not gon' bite cha. But I do want chu ta' bite me." He grabs me by my head and pushes my face down on his dick. "Suck it, Sweet Cheeks."

I try to hold my breath and suck at the same time. Useless. The foul odor suffocates me as I take his wrinkled dick in my mouth and taste his sour juices. He grabs my hair and pushes my head up and down on his dick faster and faster until he is hard again.

"Now ride me."

I pull my pink panties down and climb on top of him.

I start counting in my head. *One one thousand two one thousand three one thousand.*

"Yeah Sweet Cheeks. Work it."

Four one thousand five one thousand six one thousand.

"Yeah, I like that."

Seven one thousand eight one thousand. The tears start rolling again. There's no need to wipe because they're not going to stop until we stop. *Nine one thousand ten one thousand eleven one thousand.*

Howl, twitch, pump pump, twitch, and it's over. Twitch

pushes me off him violently like I have done him some disservice, puts his pants on, and slams the door on the way out. I hear him talking to Daddy before he leaves. Twitch is last so I soak in the tub for an hour before I go to the kitchen for the last supper.

Daddy already has his four B-12 capsules in front of him. I get him the coldest beer out of the freezer. That's the least I can do. He always chases them down with a Budweiser and I make sure I have a front row seat.

I sit at the kitchen table and watch my daddy pop his pills. I had read in my high school's library that it should take less than an hour. I eat slowly. Not wanting to miss a second of the show, I keep my eyes glued on him. He can feel me staring at him and when he looks at me, I divert my eyes and hold back a smile.

It's not over yet.

First step in the process, heavy breathing. Daddy starts taking deeper breaths. Second step, stomach cramping. He grabs his stomach, belches, and groans.

"Go get me that GasX, Girl. Bring me two."

Gladly. "Two tablets at your service and another ice cold beer." I smile. "You should be feeling all better in another fifteen minutes, Daddy." He swallows the final two tablets. My smile widens.

"What da' hell you smiling 'bout?"

He snatches my wrist and jerks me down on his lap. He pulls my face to his and begins kissing me, forcing his tongue deeply into my mouth. With his free hand, he grips my breast, which are already tender from the earlier stuff, and begins roughly squeezing them before he lets out a cry of pain. He grabs his chest and reaches for the cordless phone. Not there.

"Call 911," he gasps for air while still holding his chest.

I walk slowly to get the cordless phone out of the kitchen and then stand in front of him with the phone. At some point, he realizes that I'm not calling anybody. *Not in this lifetime.*

He tries to reach for the phone and falls to the floor moaning now in agonizing pain as the final two tablets eat away at the lining of his stomach while his heart rate is speeding to a fatal level.

From the floor, he looks up, and with his last dying breath says, "Bitch."

———

The funeral goes without incident. The burial, however, is something out of a gangsta' rap video with old ass people pouring liquor on the grave.

At the repast, all of Daddy's sisters and brothers are drunk upon arrival. I play the sad daughter too well. Everyone wants to hug and kiss me and let me know how sorry they are.

Ugh, stop fucking touching me. I finally tell them that I'm going to bed long before the company leaves. At around one in the morning, I wake up to an argument between my aunts and uncles.

"I already got three moufs ta' feed. And it ain't like Leroy left no money to take care of her. No insurance, no savings, nothing," says Aunt Margaret.

"Why it always gotta be 'bout money wit chu'? She yo' niece." says Uncle Lamart.

"Den you take her," rebuts Aunt Margaret.

Level-headed Aunt Lue fans tempers, "Okay, we not getting

nothing accomplished this way. The girl only—"

"She can come stay wit' me," says Uncle Levi.

Uncle Levi? Aw hell naw, I think. He's the only one who knows what type of stuff Daddy had me doing up in here.

"You live in a one bedroom. Where she gon' sleep?" asks Aunt Ivory.

"That's what I wanna know, uhn hun," Aunt Liz adds accusingly.

Uncle Levi, now offended asks, "Whatchu tryna say?"

I don't hear nothing else. I sneak into Daddy's room and take the safe key that he keeps hidden under the lamp on his nightstand. I go back to my room. Trying to figure out what I want to stuff in my suitcase is a waste of time.

"I don't want none of this shit."

I tiptoe out the backdoor and stop by the garage to pick up Daddy's safe. It's too heavy to carry. I look at Daddy's black and red '68 Camaro and decide I would finally get to drive that bad boy. I open the safe and take out the spare car keys. After heaving the safe in the trunk, I climb in the driver's seat and speed off. Destination, the nearest Motel 6.

———

Fucking bastard. $75, 213. Cash. Bastard. He had all this money and I had to beg for some damn sanitary napkins every time my period came.

I take the rest of the papers from the safe. A pension fund with a life-term insurance policy with me as the beneficiary, a separate $100,000 life insurance policy with me as the beneficiary, and the deed to our house that is paid for with my name as the original owner. According to the deed, I've owned it since I was three.

Wonder what my credit score is?

I look into the safe to make sure I had gotten every dollar out when I notice one more piece of paper stuck to the back wall of the safe. I pull out the old brittle sheet of paper that has what is undoubtedly a huge bourbon stain that had not only discolored the paper but also erased most of the information. I try to make out most of information, but a lot of it is all washed away.

What the fuck? No way! What does this mean?

The tears stream down my face. And they are real this time, not like the ones at the funeral. I can't stop crying. I cry myself to sleep.

Diamond Top

*Sometimes I go about pitying myself,
and all the time I am being carried on
great wings across the sky.*

—Ojibway Saying

Jazz_____
November 2005

Rebecca drags into my office sporting the charcoal grey DKNY skirt suit that I had given her last year for Secretary's Day.

The phone rings and instead of walking back to her desk in the reception area, she reaches across mine and snatches it up. "Thank you for calling the Law Offices of Attorney Jasmine Livingston. How may I help you?" Rebecca passes me my decaf vanilla latte. She pauses and listens to the caller for a few seconds before informing them that "Attorney Livingston is unavailable."

Rebecca screens all my calls because, since winning the Labotech case, my schedule has been unyielding. Taking on a

Fortune 500 pharmaceutical company can either make or break your career in this game, so I was pleased when the verdict came in.

Labotech had used plastic manufactured in a factory in China for their intravenous bags causing deadly chemicals to be released into hundreds of patients, resulting in thirteen deaths. One of the victims was a four-year old little girl. This class action suit against Labotech brought the notoriety that I need as a Black female attorney in a major metropolis like Chicago.

"Yes of course. I can give her your message when she becomes available. What company do you represent?" Rebecca scribbles the message on the pad and thanks them again for calling.

"Hey Dimples," she half smiles and greets me in the same way she has since our first year of law school.

"Hey Girlie. How was your weekend?"

"Short," she answers in a word, licks her finger, and flips through the message pad, "Mr. Brennan called. Again. Urgent message of course." She lifts up two fingers and motions to indicate that that is a quote and rolls her eyes. "Said that he raised his offer to $50,000. Asked that you return his call today because he'll be leaving the country on Wednesday for two weeks."

I take a sip of my latte and lean back in my chair. Paul Brennan had cornered me for over a half hour at Shaun's birthday party a few weeks back, trying to convince me to take on this case.

Brennan Publication has five national and two international tabloids. Killa' JoBo, the gangster rapper filing the lawsuit, has a good lawyer and a good case considering the tabloids claimed that he had sex with his youngest daughter although he has no children. Killa' JoBo's CD sales plummeted and he had to cancel several stops on his worldwide concert tour.

His company stands to lose millions if it blows this case. And, even if they win, insurance premiums will probably go through the roof, if they haven't already. That could bankrupt a company. "Call and tell him that the prices for my services are non-negotiable." *Bet he wouldn't go to Schmidt, Lorenz, & McKinley with that offer,* I think. "Be sure to thank him for considering our firm and send him out one of our 2006 calendars as a consolation. That way our number is readily accessible to him, if ever he wishes to pay for our services." *It's $100,000 or no deal.*

Rebecca jots down the message and a few extra notes as if she were a born again secretary and not a law school graduate with a Juris Doctorate. A month after we graduated from law school, Rebecca's parents died in a car accident. She failed the Bar twice and after that vowed never to take it again. Talking about some family curse or something.

As Rebecca continues to read my messages, the view of Lake Michigan off the Chicago skyline beckons me to turn my chair around. I marvel at how the Sears Tower and John Hancock Building pale in comparison to the Smurfit Stone Building. The diamond-shaped slope of the top of the structure is truly beautiful. Especially at night when the slope is outlined by white light bulbs, making it the most noticeable building in the city's skyline. That spectacular sight almost justifies it only being forty-one floors, nowhere near a skyscraper by Chicago's standards.

Swiveling back around to face her as she drones through the messages I ask, in a failed attempt not to sound frustrated or overwhelmed although I am both at that moment, "How many messages do I have?"

"Well, there were seventeen voice mails when I got here at 8:3o." Rebecca slouches her thin, lanky frame down onto the over-sized charcoal, leather lounge chair, as if she has already worked a full day.

"About fourteen or fifteen people have left messages in the two hours that I've been here. And I can't begin to tell you how many people said that they would try you back later." She puts her micro braids behind her ears revealing hoop earrings that are too big for her beady head.

The phone rings and she looks at it like it has offended her. I put a finger on each of my cheeks and raise them into a smile. Putting on a delayed smile, she answers the phone and takes another message.

She's barely cradled the phone, before it rings again along with the doorbell. "That must be your 11:00." Rebecca looks at the security monitor before buzzing them in and then she answers the phone. She pauses with a genuine smile this time.

"She's never too busy for you Ambassador Hamilton. Just one second." Rebecca puts the call on hold before she hands me the receiver.

"Rebecca, offer the women coffee or tea and biscotti and tell them I'm on a very important phone call and that I'll be with them shortly."

Two of the phone lines buzz simultaneously while she gathers her things. "See what I mean?" is her question in an exasperated huff as she rushes out the door to her desk in the reception area.

I anxiously wait for her to pull the door up before I release the hold button, "Hi, Daddy."

"Hey, Pumpkin. How's my superstar doing?"

"Good. Great. Are you back from the Ukraine?"

I can feel his smile across the continents. My daddy's voice always soothes my soul. People compare it to Barry White's. Such a gentle spirit.

I look at his picture on my desk. No smile, he's wearing his black karate uniform and black belt with ten yellow stripes on the ends. My father's a big man. About 6'5" and 300 hundred pounds. All lean. He owns the largest dojo in Chicago. That's actually how Chase and I met. My father was Chase's master.

I've never been one to get caught up in all that talk about soul mates, but that day made me a believer. I went to drop off some equipment that daddy had left at home. Because it was after hours, the doors were locked and who happened to open the door for me but the world's sexiest chocolate dream. When I looked at him, I knew he had to be the finest, most sensuous chocolate brother in the universe. *And* he was dripping in sweat. *Mmm, mmm, mmm.*

Then he smiled showing off dimples that can outshine mine any day as well as perfectly straight teeth with a narrow gap in between his two front ones. *Be still my heart.* I saw the fishing rod come out and yank me by the nose.

He was saying something to me. Yeah, his lips were moving. But I swear to this day that no sound was coming out. *Damn yo' ass is fine* was all I thought. I shimmy my shoulders and shift in my seat to try to shake off the memories that are a momentary distraction.

"We miss you so much, Daddy."

"Yeah, I know. I thought I'd be home last month, but you know how it goes. The government here is so corrupt that it's difficult to get anything accomplished without going through the bureaucratic ringer."

"And of course there's neither bureaucracy nor corruption here in the States," I counter to remind him of whence he came.

"We can only dream and pray," he sounds a little more serious than I had intended that comment to be. "So how's the practice? They covered that big case you won on the news all the way on this side of the globe. A group of European lawyers were waiting to see the outcome of your case before filing their class action suit."

"Really?" I smile. "I had heard that there were some other victims."

"Yeah. You've blazed the trail for a whole bunch of grieving families, Pumpkin. That has to make you feel good."

I grab my Cloisonné exercise balls with the Yin Yang design that Daddy brought from one of his many trips to Asia and roll them around in my left hand. I seek solace in my diamond top.

"Daddy, honestly, I haven't been able to feel anything quite yet. The firm has gone from being a two-room, two person office to needing an entire floor, support staff, and more attorneys overnight."

"Are you surprised?"

Being that I haven't admitted, not even to myself, that I'm caught off guard by the rapid progression of my practice, I reluctantly answer, "A little."

He's unable to contain his amazement. "I don't know why. Remember when you graduated from law school? You jumped right into your own practice, going against the advice of me and your mother. Finding your way. Establishing yourself. And you told me that very day that in ten years you would expand your practice and partner up with some of the best lawyers in the country to make a dynamic team."

"Yeah, I know but—"

"There were no if, ands, or buts when you started, so there can be none now. Remember our life's motto: There is no shock time available, only limited time to bask in the glory of your accomplishments, then you *must* take your throne. Are you ready to take the throne?"

I place my stress balls back in their case. "Are you ready to give it up?" is the last question I ask my daddy before I let him go.

Boo Hoo

The best executive is the one who has sense enough to pick good men to do what he wants done, and self-restraint to keep from meddling with them while they do it.

—Theodore Roosevelt

Amber_____

Where *do I begin?* My thick chestnut curls bounce and sway as I inspect my profile from left to right. Left, right. *What look do I need?* Soft and seductive or bright and vibrant. Maybe I'll do hot and sexy. Boy this is a difficult task because, according to my calculations, I am undeniably perfect.

My long, thick lashes frame my slanted onyx eyes which radiate against my latte complexion. I part my full lips and laugh at my remarkable reflection revealing the most stunning smile. *Yes flawless.* Deciding that only a select few can successfully pull off the au naturale look, I put away my Classic Pose Marilyn Monroe mirror and Milan make-up case.

I look out the window of the black Lincoln sedan. LAX is grid-locked. *Hopefully it's not like this tomorrow when I have to go back to Chicago.*

"Don't take the 405; it's a parking lot at this time of day." The driver whips pass the freeway and heads for LaBrea toward Hollywood. When the limo turns off Highland onto Hollywood Boulevard up to the main entrance of the Kodak Theatre, I glance at my watch to assure I'm on schedule.

"Back entrance," I say, wanting to avoid the crowd.

The driver whirls pass the theater and makes a right onto Orange Drive then on Franklin to circle around to the Orchid Avenue entrance where only a few high-powered people gather.

"Out front. Hour fifteen," I hop out of the Lincoln, unassisted. *This shouldn't take long.*

"Yes, Ms. Cherrington. I'll be out front."

"How many times do I have to ask you to call me Amber?" I snap and slam the door.

As I stride toward the back entrance, I look down at my low-rise palazzo pants and three-button suit jacket to make sure no wrinkles have settled in on the ride from the airport. And, of course, to make sure my belly ring is playing peek-a-boo with the world. *Yeah, you all good.*

Sporting a red blazer that matches the velvet rope that he quickly moves so as not to break my stride, the security guard briefly, but knowingly, locks eyes with me. Inside, the lights are just being dimmed in The Kaufman Theater. Before I walk inside, I put on my Versace wire rim glasses which are equipped with night lenses to balance my vision quicker than the other occupants in the room. Senator Warren is sitting in his usual seat with his customary drink in front of him. The waitress has just brought his dinner out and is placing the food down, creating a great distraction. I hurry swiftly pass them and drop the tablet into his goblet, which contains Louis XIII. The $1800 bottle of cognac is all he drinks.

Walking briskly to the front to take my seat beside the man of my dreams I chirp, "Hey You," releasing more excitement than I had intended.

"Did the flight make a smooth landing?" he asks, knowing that I would get the double meaning.

I take off my glasses and put them back in their case. Leaning over, I whisper seductively in his ear, "Whenever I'm the navigator, things will always go smoothly. You can bet on that."

Overlooking my efforts, Karob simply responds, "Wonderful Love." He grabs my hand, as he has many times before, and pecks me on my lips because, for all intensive purposes, I am his wife. If only for one night. I gaze lovingly at him. *Ain't gotta fake this.*

Karob is so beautiful that he could have been from a sculpture. Big dark curls that have a mind of their own and his smooth, radiant olive skin scream 'Touch me.' I put my hand up and caress his soft curls then let it fall down to his broad shoulders. This is the only time I get to survey his body because it is always hidden under loose fitting clothing. Now if there's a strong wind, the outline of his thigh muscles or eight-pack can be seen.

Talk about the simple pleasures of life.

Karob's strong Italian features are even more prevalent when he's in motion because his Italian gait is somewhere between confident and cocky. His father, who was Egyptian and Italian, was a member of the Italian Intelligence Agency before he mysteriously died when Karob was fourteen. After that, the entire family was sent to the States and put in protective custody. He's never returned to Italy.

The only feature that he probably inherited from his beautiful Moroccan mother whose picture he keeps in his wallet is the smooth hand that is holding mine as the documentary begins. I switch my focus as hard as that is.

The Tsunami Creation is an intriguing forty-five minute presentation on global warming's effect on the world's huge bodies of water. The producer is presenting to major investors to get funding for the final phase of the project.

When the lights come up and the applause ceases, the producer waits a few minutes to give the uninterested viewers time to leave before he begins his presentation. His assistants have already begun passing out the media kits when Karob and I make our way out. We find seats with an unobstructed view of the Kaufman Theatre's entrance and look into each other's eyes.

"Yes, the deposit has been made," he speaks gazing intently in my eyes with a smile. I giggle as if he were a witty jokester. He licks his lips dramatically as he listens to the voice from the microchip planted in his ear.

Now that's a bit much you sexy mothafucka, I think.

He continues, "Current status is presently unknown due to the, uh.....standby for an update."

As if on cue, Senator Warren is escorted out of the theatre.

"Honey, are you alright?" asks Mrs. Warren.

"I think I have a little heartburn," the senator responds. "I just need to lie—" Senator Warren grabs his chest and keels over.

Daammn! Four hundred pounds fall hard.

Several people run to assist as his wife yells, "Call 911! Please, someone call 911!"

"Jorge, go get the defibrillator," barks the manager. "He's having a heart attack."

Jorge runs to the office adjacent the theatre to get the device. Karob and I stroll casually over to where a small gathering has formed and join the other onlookers. Jorge breaks through the crowd with the defibrillator and hits the power button. Unfortunately for the senator, there is no charge. He works quickly to get the machine on.

"I think the battery's dead."

"Go to my office and grab the other one off the charger," yells the manager as he performs CPR.

Doesn't matter. That one won't be working either.

By that time, it's too late.

Your time has expired, I think as we watch Senator Warren gasp for that last breath of air and close his eyes. *Good riddance.*

Karob and I walk slowly towards the Kodak Theatre exit with Mrs. Warren in the background screaming like a banshee.

Boo fucking hoo, I think, immediately tuning out her wails.

"Yes Sir. Mission is complete, Sir," Karob updates. We dodge in and out of the tourists.

"No makeup, huh?" he says without looking at me. "That's a good look for you."

I smile. I had made the right choice.

———

I pull the covers of the California King bed up to my chin. *Damn hotel rooms are always cold.* I flip through the cable news channels. All the major networks have coverage of the senator's death, linking his heart attack to a highly-publicized, botched-up triple bypass that he had last year. I stop on Fox Cable News.

Just then there's a knock on my hotel door. I walk to the door and look out to see Karob with his curls hidden underneath a baseball cap. *Lord have mercy on my soul.* I run my hands over my hair to flatten any stray strands and open the door.

He's changed out of his suit and is wearing a blue and white Nike jogging suit with matching leather tennis shoes. *And I thought I was sexy.*

He passes me two greasy paper bags. "Figured you'd be hungry."

"I am. Whatcha bring?" I try not to sound too, *too* excited, but the truth of the matter is, I may not make it another five seconds without screaming, "Go Amber. It's ya' birthday. We gon' party like it's ya' birthday."

"Well a birdie tells me that your favorite dish is Shrimp in Lobster Sauce."

"Oh, so you checking up on me, huh?" I smile and switch over to the table with a bit more 'umph' in my step.

"Just a little." He returns the smile. That breath-taking smile makes me wanna change everything bad about myself and be the woman he could love unconditionally.

We sit at the table in the corner and begin to eat. He grabs the remote off the bed and flips to *Good Times*. It's the episode when Penny's mother is abusing her and Wilona saves her.

"I love this episode," I say.

"Me too."

Let the Games Begin

Only one man in 1000 is a leader of men.
The other 999 follow women.

—Groucho Marx.

Jazz____

"Send them in, Rebecca."

The three men enter my office wearing expensive black suits, overpriced cufflinks, and shoes shining so tough that they must have gotten them shined downstairs in my lobby. I walk around the desk and give them all a nice firm handshake, making sure I grip their hands tighter than they do mine.

"John, Mitch, Tom. Good to see you."

I suppress the urge to hug my childhood friends because right now this is strictly business. For as long as I could remember, our fathers had golfed together, traveled together, and did whatever politicking that had to be done—on and off the golf course.

Rumor has it, that the four of our fathers along with some other men, are the pulse of the city. This legend has thirteen or fourteen members. They meet twice a month for a "poker game." And, although none of them are city politicians, they allegedly control many of the election outcomes with their directives, dealings, and dollars. Of course, Daddy denies this.

We make small talk for about five or ten minutes, and when I see Tom give Mitch the eye, I ask, "Can I offer you anything before we get started? Coffee, water, juice?" *A shot of bourbon?*

"No, no, we're fine," John says.

Because Mitch and I lived on the same block all of our lives and are both graduates of the University of Iowa Law School, I figure he will take the lead. I'm right.

"Pretty impressed with your practice," Mitch says.

I smile and nod.

"Well, we want to make you an offer." He begins talking with his hands as he often does when he's nervous. "Now hear us out before you make any decisions."

"Of course," I say with an inquisitive look on my face although I know what they want. John's wife is friends with Shaun's assistant. So Shaun told Asia and Asia, of course, immediately told me. I prepared my game plan.

"We want to buy your practice," Mitch says and seems to have stopped breathing as he evaluates my reaction." When it doesn't come fast enough for him, he continues, "And you don't have to worry because we'll maintain the highest level of integrity. And if you like, you can stay on and work for us."

If Chase were here, he'd have asked him if he was on dope or dog food. But instead I ask, "What's your offer?"

He pulls a cream envelope out of his breast pocket and hands it to me. I take the linen card out of the envelope and look at the embroidered figure.

Gahdamn, am I worth $7 million already? I wonder. "Do you actually think I would sell my practice for this measly amount of money?" I am able to say in a voice stronger than I knew I had. I thought I would choke on the words. "We've known each other too long for such an insult," I add.

"Well, the figure is somewhat adjustable," says John whose father is the wealthiest out of all of our fathers, and I'm sure the mastermind behind this entire plan. *Ooh, wait 'til I tell Daddy this.*

They are all looking at me again, waiting on a reply. I spin my chair around and look at my diamond roof top. Inhaling deeply before exhaling loudly, I walk to the window and look out as if I am in deep thought.

When I finally turn around, I must have caught them off guard because Mitch jumps and has to look up from my legs. Now, John doesn't have as far to go. He only has to look up from my butt. *You men are so predictable.*

I walk around the desk and take the seat directly across from Mitch. I sit up parochial school straight, but slowly cross my legs public school style. *Eyes up here boys.* "So this is negotiable?" I ask while waving the embroidered linen card in their direction.

"Absolutely. Definitely. Yes," is the scattered answers.

"And we certainly understand if you need to talk it over with Chase before you make any major decisions," John offers.

Like you talked it over with your big mouthed wife? I think not. I lean on the arm of the chair and put my finger underneath my chin. "Since this is negotiable, I have a suggestion." I rub my chin with my finger. "Maybe you can buy into my firm and we can become partners."

They all look at each other like they didn't know what to do. Like they hadn't come up with a contingency plan if that option were brought to the table. I mean, really, there are not that many plausible outcomes for this scenario. *Come on guys, you have to be better prepared than this.*

"Uh, well, I guess we can do some number crunching on that and get back to you later," John says while looking for assistance from Tom and Mitch.

Seeing that they are thrown off of their square, I suggest, "Why don't we do it now. I've already blocked out a couple of hours for this meeting. That way we can cut down on the back and forth of the negotiation process."

They all look skeptical. Nervous eyes move between the three of them with no one taking the lead. John takes out his handkerchief and wipes his forehead, Mitch shifts in his seat, and Tom massages the back of his neck.

"You're already here so we might as well move forward on this. What do you have to lose?"

"I guess you're right," Tom finally concedes.

"Good. Now, you guys know that Bill O'Connor's office is across the hall and he's the best accountant in Chicago. He even has his J.D., although he doesn't practice." Bill's father is another one of the "poker players", so we all know him as well. "Rebecca, can you get Bill on the phone for me, please?"

Rebecca has Bill on the phone instantly and I put him on speaker. "Bill. How are you?"

"I'm doing great. But I'm sure not as good as Chicago's super counselor. You are all anyone talks about in the legal circles these days."

"Oh, Bill, you lie like a rug."

"Oh, so that wasn't you I saw featured in the People Section of the Chicago Tribune last week? You have to be high society, inner circle, Pulitzer-prize potential *or something* to even get recommended for that section of the paper. I hear they're doing some shifting in their legal department and the youngest attorney to ever make the review board's list in their 150 year history is you. They—"

"Uh Bill, I hate to cut you off," I interject after I see my visitors' interest has been thoroughly peaked. "I'm sitting here with Tom, John, and Mitch and we wouldn't want to bore them with the workings of the Chicago Tribune."

"Oh, of course not. I certainly understand."

"I knew you would. Well, the reason I'm calling is to see if you had a little time right now to figure out some numbers for us."

"You guys are in luck. My noon appointment just called to reschedule. We'll come right over."

In less than five minutes, Bill walks into my office followed by his secretary and assistant. For better accommodation, we move to the conference table where the negotiations begin.

After I tell Bill what we're trying to figure out, he says, "Okay, I need three things from both companies: Number one, your net income for the past three years; number two, your average earnings per case for that time; and number three, your earning per quarter."

I didn't make as much as Mitch's crew did the first year that we evaluated. But I did match the second year and exceeded theirs in the third year even without the Labotech case.

After I'm convinced they know how valuable I am, I say, "I know what it's worth to me to let someone buy into my firm versus hiring extra attorneys to work for me. And I'm sure that the three of you know how much you're willing to spend. So being fair and honest, put your best offer on the table and I'll either accept it or reject it."

Their offering price is more than sufficient. Agreeing on the firm's name isn't as easy, though. I would have preferred Livingston & Associates, but we settle on Livingston, Bolden, Kelly & Bryant Law Offices, no one being completely satisfied with their name placement.

Mitch stands up with a silly smirk on his face and says, "Since all of the technicalities are out of the way, I have one thing that is *not* up for negotiation."

"Sure Mitch. What you got?" I ask as we all look at Mitch with a mixture of curiosity and confusion on our faces.

"Well, this merger creates a need for more space. And since neither of our offices will be big enough to accommodate the company's growth potential, I reserved leasing rights to the top floor of the Smurfit Stone Building."

My head spins around to look out the window at the source of my daily admiration. As I look at the diamond top, I can't contain my joy. It creeps up in my bones before it crosses my face.

This is going to be a great partnership, I think before I shake everyone's hand and walk them to the elevator.

After I come back into the office, I look at the wall clock. Shoot, it's almost five. He better not had left. I pick up the phone and dial the number. On the fourth ring, he answers the phone.

"What took you so long?" he whispers.

"How much time I got?" I find myself whispering too although no one can hear me.

"I have to put the files back in a half hour because they'll be looking to shred them."

"Be there in fifteen," I grab my keys and rush out the office.

I get there in ten minutes. He takes me to the custodial closet where the files are tucked behind an industrial size box of baking powder. What they would need baking soda for here, is beyond me. He passes me the files.

I grab my pocket flashlight out of my purse, turn it on, and hold it in my mouth. I take out my digital camera and open the first folder. I adjust the flashlight in my mouth so that it is directly on the papers and snap the pictures one at a time. Then I take my portable printer out of my bag, sit it on the shelf, and plug in the USB cord. I print out two copies of the files, just in case something happens. I put one set into an envelope addressed to myself and seal it.

"Thanks, I owe you one," I nod at him standing in the shadows of the closet.

"If you can make this happen, that will be payment enough," he winks at me.

I peek out of the closet to make sure the coast is clear before leaving. Outside, I drop the envelope into the nearest mailbox and hail a cab.

Let the games begin.

Not on
my Watch

Blood is thicker than water.
—17th Century English Proverb

Chase ____

"**S**hit!" I yell and jerk up in my bed. Three fucking a clock.
This dream is starting to piss me off.

I look at Jazz sleeping peacefully. And naked. Truly God's
masterpiece.

I ease my way out of the bed, put on my robe, and decide to do
some painting. When I open up the door to my studio, I instantly
feel stress-free. The tension that had entered my back and neck
during my recurring nightmare is gone. The hard-on that I had
while I was looking at Jazz's perfect naked body has deflated.

I look around the room that Jazz has designated as my studio
so that I wouldn't make a mess all around the house. The walls had

been white, but when they became splattered with paint, I decided to make them my swatch test. So now, every time I want to try out a new color or mixture of colors, I just slap it on the wall.

The beautiful hardwood floors have been covered with sheet paper and another layer of wood because Jazz wants to protect the floor. Protect it from what, I don't know. I keep telling her that paint cleans up, but she ain't hearing me.

I grab one of the cotton poncho cover-ups that hang on wall hooks by the door and pull it over my head. I'm in another world. Until my cell phone rings, that is.

No good news comes at three in the morning. I look at the caller id and quickly flip the phone on, "Ma, what's wrong?"

"Baby, I'm sorry ta' call ya' so late, but I couldn't sleep fa' thinking 'bout dem police who been coming round here everyday looking fa' Malik. Talking 'bout dey wanna question him 'bout some dead gurl. My baby ain't kilt nobody. He may have done a lotta bad things in his day, but he ain't never kilt nobody. I know my baby."

Dead girl? What dead girl? I wonder. "Okay, slow down Momma. Calm down and tell me what happened."

"Well, Mrs. Franklin next do' called me at work on Friday to tell me dat da' police had been coming by here everyday dis week. Well on Sunday, when I come back from church, dey wuz waiting on my po'ch. All kicked up like dey live here or something."

"How many were there?" I ask trying to get a visual so that I can know how mad I should really be.

"Two."

"Black or White?"

"One Black, one Mexican or something. Anyway, I axed da

gentlemen real nice like, 'What can I do fa' ya' officers?' Dey gon'
get all snippety wit' me and da' Black one gon' say—you know it's
always the Black one who gotta' be indignant, 'Where's dat crack
head son of yours?' Who dey think dey is?"

Mmm, mmm, mmm. Mothafuckas. "Ma, did you get the names
and badge numbers?"

"You know I did. Officer Washington and Menendez out of da'
31st Precinct. Dey thought I didn't know my rights, see. Humph.
Saying dey wuz gon' search my house. 'Not without a search
warrant,' I told dem. Den dey said dat dey don't need no warrant
when looking fa' a murder suspect. So I told dem, Den break the
do' down.' And I turned and walked to da' bus stop."

"Ma, I know the sergeant of that precinct. Get some rest and
I'll handle this. I'll call you later on today and let you know what's
going on."

"Okay, love ya' baby. Call me."

Squeezing my cell phone tightly, I look down surprised it
doesn't break in half. *I'd be goddamned if I let some pigs harass my
mother. Not on my watch.*

I go to my easel, lift a canvas off the floor onto it, and begin
painting with no objective in mind. The sun is beaming through
my blinds by the time I finish the painting.

A murder scene, identifiable by five sketched outlines, stares
back at me. Inside each outline lies a pool of blood and a police
badge. A lone shooter is in the shadows behind a brick building
with a smoking gun. No facial features are distinguishable. Just
his satisfied lips curled into a smile.

I take the black paint and brush it across the canvas. Just as I
am covering up the last pool of blood, Jazz walks in.

"There you are. I reached over to cuddle with you before I got up and you weren't there."

She smells of vanilla and lavender and is still warm from the shower. She rolls up on her tiptoes and kisses me gently on my lips then looks at my canvas, "What are you painting, a lunar eclipse?"

"That may not be a bad idea," I laugh at her joke. "Naw, it just didn't turn out right, so I had to get rid of it."

"Why didn't you just use the canvas cleaner?"

"I decided it'd look better as an eclipse." We laugh as I take off the poncho and hang it on its hook. I take her hand to lead her out of the studio into the kitchen.

"Want banana caramel pancakes or cinnamon apple pancakes?" I wash my hands and take the turkey bacon and brown eggs out of the refrigerator.

"Just eggs and toast is fine with me."

I whip the breakfast together in less than ten minutes. We eat and arrange our weekly date. We had agreed before we got married that we would never get too busy to go out on a date at least once a week. So every Monday, I ask her out as if we are still single and she lets me know if she's available or not.

"I think Friday will probably be the best day for a date. I don't know if moving from my old office to the new office will be as smooth as I would like. I ordered all new furniture that should have been there last week, but when Rebecca went to do her final inspection of the office, there was still stuff that had not been delivered—like my desk and chair."

Jazz rolls her eyes, shakes her head, and sips her freshly squeezed orange and pineapple juice. "Then some of our files are already mixed up."

I walk behind her as she continues to grumble about her arrangements. Massaging her shoulders and neck seems to slow down her complaining.

"In our contract, it clearly states that open cases are not part of the deal. There's stuff that they don't need to see. Things they can't see," is her last complaint before she goes silent. I dig my fingers deeper into the lumps that have formed on her shoulders in the past couple of months. I feel the tension leave her body.

After she finishes her last piece of cinnamon toast, I pick up her car keys and hit the automatic starter so that the car will be warm when she gets in it. I help her with her coat.

Wrapping my arms around her in a gentle hug I ask, "Need anything else, Baby?"

"No, I'll be fine. I'll call you in a little bit to let you know how things are coming."

"Things'll be coming, the same way they always do when it comes to you—perfect," I kiss her forehead before she walks out the door. "Love you, Baby," I wave.

She turns around and blows me a kiss. I leap in the air to catch it. We both laugh.

The Ida B's

I don't measure a man's success by how
high he climbs, but how high he bounces
when he hits the bottom.

—General George S. Patton

Chase_____

Jazz isn't at the end of the block before the soft sprinkles from
the dual showerhead is rolling down my body. Need to make a
phone call and a stop before my meeting with the people at the
DuSable Museum about my month long exhibit. I take State Street
to Pershing Ave., then drive east on Pershing. When I pass
Wendell Phillips High School, I know that I'm getting close. I can't
remember where my turn is, so I slowly circle the Ida B. Wells
housing projects.

My grandfather, who was active in having the Ida B's built in
1941, lived in these projects for fifty years until he died. When
they sent the housing plan to Washington D.C. in 1934, my grand-

father was a prominent member of the planning committee for the low cost housing project in the Black community.

The Ida B's are not high rise projects like the Robert Taylor Homes or Cabrini Green, but two-level town homes. I can see where the Ida B's could have been nice back in the day.

But look at them now. The place is worse than I remember. Looks like a tornado hit the Midwest and dumped all the shit right here on 39th Street. There is trash in the streets, on the sidewalk, in the grassless yards, and on the porches.

And not just paper. Cans, 40-ounce malt liquor bottles, Jay's potato chip bags, tires, shoes, whatever. And of course, nothing would be complete without your neighborhood wine head or crack addict sorting through them.

Ida B. Wells. Boy, how we honor our great heroes.

I finally decide to ask one of the graveyard shift drug dealers to help me out. I roll down the window of my '86 Accord that I use to transport paint and equipment and yell at the boy in the most aggressive voice that I can muster up at seven in the morning, "Hey, where can I find Reverend Pookie?"

The little thug takes his left hand out of the warmth of his pocket long enough to grab his dick while keeping his right hand firmly inside around what I'm sure was his overnight protection. "Who axing?"

"Yo' momma," I respond and put my hand on my visor and steady it there, letting him know that he's not the only one who keeps a little nudge at the fingertips.

The teenage boy stoops down a little to look at me then walks up to my car. He surveys the back seat, looks at me again, and then spits on the ground. "Well, you don't smell like 5-o. If you are, you won't make it out alive."

I want to get out and make him taste my 13 ½'s. But since a ass whuppin' wasn't scheduled in, I take his directions and push on. *Punk's still too young to know about my reign.*

I park my car taking care to miss the bottles that are in the gutter. After surveying the area, I get out and I walk up to the door, knocking with the secret code.

The door flings open. Reverend Pookie's eighteen-year old flavor of the month stands staring at me in a pair of sheer bright red panties with a matching camisole and a weave redder than that.

"Yeah?" she says in the raspy voice of a life-time smoker.

"Tell Reverend Pookie that Chay Chay is here to see him."

Looking me up and down like I'ma pork chop tempting a starving bulldog, she takes her hand and puts it on my chest and rubs down to the muscles in my stomach, "Chay Chay, huh. I'll tellum ya here, Chay Chay."

She moves to let me in, closes the door, and then conveniently drops something on the floor. She bends down slowly and rolls back up even slower, looking back to see if I take the bait. Ignoring her blatant display of seduction, I'm already at the couch sitting down.

Don't do kids. Didn't do kids when I was a kid.

She walks upstairs and comes back down with Reverend Pookie. He's wearing a black silk robe with a tiger sprawled around from front to back. His cornrolls are neatly prepared in some intricate juvenile design that is in sharp contrast with the gray hairs that are popping up all over his head, but in full alignment with the braces that he has on his teeth. *Thank God, he's fixing that Flava' Flav grill.*

"Well, well, well. Look wut da' wind den blew in. Chase." He gives me a brother man hug and dap. "What brings you ta' dis side of town?" He plops down on the couch. And before I can answer him, the girl kneels down in front of him, opens his robe, puts her head in his lap, and begins bobbing up and down. He closes his eyes and leans back on the couch to give her a better angle.

This mothafucka must think we still gang banging in high school.

"I need to talk to you."

"Talk. I'm listening," he grabs the girl's head and pushes it down further in his lap without opening his eyes.

I should reach over and slap the shit outta him.

"Alone."

He looks at me and then down at his life-size Barbie doll. "Oh her. Don't worry about Red Hot. She deaf in one ear and can't hear out the other," he laughs as the girl continues like she's deaf for real. When he sees that I'm not amused, he reluctantly taps the girl on the shoulder. "Baby, I need to talk some business right now. We'll finish this up in a minute. In a Red Hot minute," he smiles at her.

She gets off her knees and passionately kisses him before walking off.

When she's outta earshot, I say, "Know them cops Washington and Menendez?"

"Oh yeah. They infamous 'round here for rough ups and shake downs. Wut 'bout 'em?" he has a suspicious look on his face.

I look him straight in the eyes, "The possum had squirrel for dinner."

He quickly looks away as if me and my words would disappear if he doesn't see me. Reverend Pookie walks to the window and pulls the curtain back to look outside. "Are you sure 'bout that?"

That's a good damn question, I think but what comes out my mouth is, "Yeah, I'm positive."

He seems to marinate on the idea for a long time as if the request is optional. "Then consider it done," he responds like he thinks he *for real* had a choice.

Reverend Pookie turns around and tries covering the bulge in his robe. "Now I got to run upstairs before my dick explodes." He takes both hands and tries pushing it down. "Her little ass keeps my dick hard. Oooh weeee! Red Hot." He smiles revealing all the metal in his mouth. "You ain't need nuttin' else did cha, Man?"

"Naw, that's it."

He holds the door open for me. "Well don't be no stranger. My do' always open."

"Aiight Man."

Taking the same way out as in, I slow down when I get to the teenage boy's post. I roll down my window to see if the lil' thug needs the history lesson that's engraved on the bottom of my Timberlands, but upon further inspection, I realize that they have changed shifts. This is a different, sagging-pants thug.

I drive off a little happier because a coat of snow has begun to cover some of the shit in the streets.

Pie in Silence

By the time the fool has learned the
game, the players have dispersed.

—Ashanti Proverb

Asia____

"Asia......Asia," my sister, India, shakes me out of a peaceful
sleep. "Get dressed and get your *butt* downstairs. Mom and
Dad are waiting on us."

I look at the clock on the nightstand. Oh shit! *It's a quarter to
midnight.* I have ten minutes. "Where's Shaun?" I ask but India
is already out the door.

I run to the closet, take out my red linen Gucci pants suit, and
lay it on the bed. I try to decide between Gucci sandals or Gucci
boots and figure I'd save that for last. *Thank God I showered before
I took my nap.*

I sit at the vanity that my mother had given me for my 12th
birthday and begin to apply my face, working quickly in light of

the time restraints placed on me.

See in my family, we have a New Year's Eve tradition. Every year on the eve of New Year's Eve, we all fly to my parent's home in Los Angeles. The entire family talks about what has happened over the year. Any blessings, tragedies, or advice is put on the table so that everyone can start the New Year fresh and uninhibited by last year's old news.

I look in the mirror. *Not bad for a rush job.* I throw on my clothes and sandals, grab my matching Gucci purse, then run out of my childhood room. As I descend the spiraling staircase, I hear my father's deep belly laugh and I know the festivities have begun.

In the family room, I immediately look around for Shaun, but he's not here. Everyone else is though. My parents and grand-parents, as well as India and her husband, Ralph. Then there's my Uncle Robert and his wife, Helen along with their son, Jason and Layla, his girlfriend. I walk over to India and ask where Shaun is.

"Left around 9:30."

"Really? Did he say where he was going?"

"Didn't ask." India says matter of factly and gives me that "big sister knows best" glare.

I hate it when she acts like she knows so much more than me. She's only two years older. I wish she'd get over herself. Plus, she's not really a "big" big sister as she always likes to remind me. People have always thought we were twins. We looked identical growing up. But that all changed when I married a diamond deal-er and she married a car dealer. Now we live in two different worlds. Mine laced with objects, events, and status that wealth brings. And hers sprinkled with whatever lowly things that middle class people must settle for.

India's been pretty disgusted by Shaun's frequent absences and extended business trips. Sometimes, I just call her to vent. You know, like sisters do. Well, she gets so mad, cursing and yelling at me to leave Shaun and come home. So unnecessary. She has no good reason to suggest that I leave my husband. Because he works all the time? Because he's out late? I usually make up an excuse to get off the phone because she's so irate. I can never understand why it bothers her so much. She just doesn't understand the dedication needed to meet our goals, so I stopped trying to explain it to her. She's never going to like my husband because I have the better husband. And she knows it.

I sit on the sofa next to her and listen to the brewing conversation. Finally, my father stands up to give the ceremonial opening speech that officially begins the discussions. "This year, the family has been blessed. There are no deaths or illnesses, no debilitating accidents or conditions." My father pauses and holds his head down, "But let's take a moment of silence for the people who could not be with us this year."

We all bow our heads in remembrance of Uncle Timothy, my father's youngest brother, who died in a freak skiing accident. And my Aunt Martha, whose sudden death from lymphatic cancer almost killed my mother.

After that everyone tells of their happy progressions over the year. India is finally pregnant, after trying for six years. Jason's girlfriend, Layla, is now his fiancée. They're getting married next year. My father is retiring from the California Supreme Court so that he and my mother can travel the world. Everybody's life seems to be great.

"And what about you, Sugarplum? How was your year?" Granny asks, calling me by my childhood nickname. "Everything has been absolutely wonderful," I smile looking at each of my family members. "We bought the condo next door to ours and knocked out the wall for more living space, went to Madrid for two weeks for our anniversary, and we started a foundation this year for abandoned infants. Life is good," I throw my arms out in front of me. "Shaun is the absolute best."

Everyone is silent for a minute before Uncle Robert asks, "So where is he now? If everything is on the up and up, and you two have had such a absolutely wonderful time this year, why isn't he here holding your hand and partaking in this family tradition?" He only pauses long enough to make his eyes bulge out like a wanna be Bernie Mac. "Everyone else is here and you sitting there looking like a sick widow or something."

I don't know what to say. I just look around for someone to defend me, but when my dad weighs in on the subject, all he says is, "I'm going to have to agree with your Uncle Robert on this one. Shaun's been in the family long enough to know how important this is. If he's not here, Sweetie, it's because he doesn't want to be here."

"I'm sure there is a perfectly good reason why he's not here. Business has picked up so much lately that he's become extremely busy." I search the room for a sympathetic face, a pair of understanding eyes. Nothing. "There was a new mine discovered in the Namib Desert in Africa with very rare diamonds and—"

"No excuse," my father uses the umpire's safe signal for emphasis. "I've had to make life-altering rulings over the years that

I deferred to different dates because I knew that family comes first."

"But, Daddy, it doesn't bother me that he works all the time. For the lifestyle that we want to maintain, it's necessary that he puts in a lot of hours."

"See, I told you," India leans towards our mother and whispers loud enough for everyone to hear, "Da' Nile ain't just a river in Egypt."

I spin my head around so fast that a bunch of my hair goes into my mouth. "I am not in denial about anything!" I yell while removing the strands. "Just because Ralph cheated on you with that stripper doesn't mean that everyone's husband is messing around," I add without remorse.

"Asia!" my mother yells at me in shock because this is a tidbit of information that India failed to tell her.

"That was really low, Asia," India gets up and storms out of the room. I'm sure she runs out to keep from slapping the crap out of me. I've been known to go for the jugular in the past and it always ends with her knee in my chest and hands around my neck. I was never a big fighter. Ralph follows behind her.

My mother snaps at me. "That was uncalled for. If you're going to be mad, you need to be mad at the person who's mistreating you—not the people who love you."

I want to say that I'm sorry, but since I'm not, I don't.

"Does that make you feel better now? You want someone else to hurt?" my mother asks.

Rhetorical. So I don't answer. I want to leave too, but if India's on the other side of the door, not even the growing baby inside of her will keep her from laying hands on me.

Granny walks over to me and holds my hand. "Sweetie, all of us have had rocky roads and dry patches." She seems to be the only one in the room who cares about my feelings.

"Amen to that," agrees my father as he reaches out and takes my mother's hand.

"And none of us are immune to boredom in our relationships." Granny caresses my face with the back of her hand. "But if you can't admit that something's wrong, you're not going to be able to fix the problem."

"And if the problem is something other than boredom," my grandfather interjects, "it may be time for some counseling. Because even if he's working as much as he claims he is, nobody throws themselves into their job like that for no reason."

Not you too Grandpa.

The door flings open and slams against the wall. Shaun stumbles in. His white shirt, one side tucked in and the other hanging out, has a brown stain on the front and is wrinkled. His tie is twisted to the side and it looks like his jacket may be inside out.

"I didn't miss the party did I?" Shaun practically spits every word out and sounds like his tongue is too big for his mouth.

"No Honey, we were all wondering where you were. I told them that you probably had a business meeting." I go over to kiss him on his cheek as India and Ralph come back in the room holding hands.

"Remember I told you that the Sultan was in Los Angeles for the New Year and wanted to discuss a ten-year exclusive contract. I couldn't miss this opportunity." He takes off his jacket which is definitely on inside out.

"Does the Sultan wear red lipstick?" India asks pointing to the lipstick on his collar and sleeve.

"Oh that." Shaun rubs the lipstick deeper into his white shirt-sleeve. "Some lady had too much to drink and passed out and I just happened to be the one close enough to catch her. I may have to send her my dry cleaning bill," Shaun laughs.

India continues, "And does the Sultan require that you miss these two belt hoops in the back? Nah, naw, that's okay. Strike that one. Is it fashionable where the Sultan comes from to have a *used* condom stuck to the side of your pants?"

Everyone looks down at Shaun's pants leg. Sure enough, there is a condom hanging there with gooey stuff on it.

"Huuu" I gasp in disbelief along with a number of different sounds, sighs, and grunts that come from across the room.

"What do you have to say to that?" India asks and I can't tell if she's talking to me or Shaun.

"I don't know where that came from," Shaun reaches down to remove the condom.

"Well don't touch it. You don't know who could have been using that." I grab a napkin off the table and hand it to him.

"You don't know who could have been using that?!" India is hollering at this point. "He knows who was using it and everybody in here knows who was using it except for the airhead in the room—that would be you if your valley girl brain couldn't figure that out either." India is keeping it on a personal level.

While trying to keep his balance, Shaun looks at India and blinks a couple of times before he asks, "What crawled up yo' ass and died?"

"Shaun! What's gotten in to you? Come on, you've had too much to drink. Let me get you cleaned up," I take his arm and try to lead him out of the family room, although I'm a little happy that he's coming to my defense. He snatches away from me. "Naw! She's been riding me for a couple of years now. What? You wish this condom had yo' juices on it?"

I cover my mouth at his outburst.

"ENOUGH!" Daddy yells as the rest of us try to pick our mouths up off the floor. "Lady's out of the room!" He points to the door. "The men are going into conference."

All the women groan at that announcement because we know that when the men have a conference, they take an oath of secrecy. Nothing leaves the room, not the topic of discussion, outcomes, or admissions. Not to mention that it usually lasts until morning.

"Ladies, let's head to the kitchen and have some of my lemon meringue pie," my mother offers.

Normally, we would have been elated about eating the dessert that has won my mother many pie baking competitions, but not tonight. We all walk out disgusted by the eviction. The double maple doors shut behind us.

In the kitchen, my mother turns on the kettle, takes the pie out of the refrigerator, and slices everyone a piece. We eat our pie in silence. When the teakettle whistles, I jump. India must have taken that as the beginning of the race because she leaps right in and says, "I guess I'll address the pink elephant in the room."

The Power of Who You Know

Keep your friends close and your enemies closer.

—unknown

Asia____

No words are spoken as Shaun and I drive to Crustacean Seafood Cuisine in Beverly Hills. I want to ask him what they talked about last night, but I know it's useless. Could tell him what they said about him, but I don't want to upset him. I want to kiss him, but I don't know if that's appropriate either. So we just ride. It's a relief to finally pull up at valet.

Walking into Crustacean is always so soothing. The entryway to the restaurant pours into the bar and the clear glass floor aquarium leads into the dining area. I look down at the array of tropical fish swimming beneath my feet and feel like a weight has been lifted off of me. Temporarily anyway.

The host immediately escorts us to our table. Small talk assuages ill-feelings from last night. All except for India's. She doesn't look at me the whole time. When I ask her to pass me the creamer, she does so without an utterance, even after I say thank you.

I nibble on the calamari without adding much to any of the discussions that evening. I just wish that today was tomorrow so that I'd be at home in my bed without people accusing my husband of all these awful things.

This has to be up there with the three worse holidays in my life. Nothing can top this, I think.

That is until I glance over to the bar and my worse nightmare is motioning for me to come to the restroom. I immediately excuse myself. I must have been too abrupt because India and my mother exchange glances. But I didn't have time to worry about that.

"I need to make a run to the little girl's room. Be back in a bit."

Crustacean has a single restroom for women and one for men, so I wait patiently behind the four other women in line. When it is our turn, we go in together.

"What are you doing here, Amber?" I try to keep my voice down so that the people on the other side of the door won't hear me.

"I decided that I didn't want to be cold on New Year's Eve ever again. So I took a trip," Amber says while touching up her bronze Mac lipstick and then adding the gloss.

"And this is the only place you could think to come, huh?"

"Asia, I didn't come here to argue or upset you," she says sounding more sincere than I expect from her. Her sincerity unnerves me, so I wait for the other shoe to drop. And it does.

"Since I'm here, you might as well introduce me. That *is* your family, right?"

"When hell freezes over," I reach for the door handle.

Amber holds it closed, "Either you introduce me or I'll introduce myself, but I will not spend New Year's Eve alone."

"You didn't think about that before you flew 2000 miles away from home?"

"Yeah, I did," is the only answer she offers as her smirk turns into a full-blown smile. I want to smack that self-assured smirk off her face.

Amber prances behind me like the *fucking* Queen of Sheba as we walk over to the table where my entire immediate family dines. *Which one of the gods did I offend this time?*

At the table, I stand behind my father trying to formulate my words, "Hey everyone, I want you to meet someone. This is uh.....a friend from Chicago who just so happened to be standing in line for the ladies room with me." I do my best Vanna White hand motion. "Amber, family. Family, Amber."

"Well hi. How...." my mother stops mid-sentence when she turns to meet Amber. Then she just looks at Amber like maybe she is the fucking Queen of Sheba before she finishes her sentence in a sing song way. "How are you?" My mother smiles.

"God, you are *absolutely* gorgeous," Amber starts laying it on thick with her first line. "You must be Asia's mother. The striking resemblance is uncanny." She looks back and forth between me and my mother. "You actually look young enough to be her sister."

"Well thank you, Dear," my mother grins like she doesn't hear that all the time.

"And you must be her father." My father leans back in his chair enchanted by Amber's smile. "Asia tells me that you're not only a judge, but a California Supreme Court Justice with several published books. She gave me two of them as a Christmas gift and I've actually finished one of them already."

I cringe. *The little lying witch had done her research.* And that's one way to peak my father's interest is to talk about his books.

"Really? Which one did you read?" he asks as Amber eagerly sits in the empty seat next to Daddy.

"I read *The Climb to Supreme.* It was so enlightening that I decided to go to law school after I finish next year at UIC in Chicago."

"You don't say," Daddy smiles.

Amber nods, "I actually came to L.A. looking for an internship because in Chicago, everything is so corrupt and political that you have to know somebody to get into some of the bigger firms."

"Well we know somebody," Shaun offers unaware that I am vigorously shaking my head.

"Really?" Amber asks.

"Yeah. You remember Jasmine who was sitting at the table with us at my birthday party a few months ago."

"Yes of course. Jasmine and Chase, the couple who look like newlyweds although they've been married for a while. I remember them."

"Well, Jasmine's firm just merged with some other big time attorneys and probably needs an intern or even better, a paralegal. I'm sure I can pull a few strings and make that happen for you."

I jump in hoping to terminate the conversation before it gets out of hand, "And *I'm sure* Amber would prefer to earn her opportunities through her own efforts instead of having them handed to her by a bunch of strangers."

"It's obvious that you haven't read your father's book," Amber says while wagging a well-manicured finger at me. "The title of Chapter 17 is 'Never Underestimate the Power of Who You Know.' Truly Informational."

But you don't know no damn body.

"That's absolutely correct," Dad chimes in. "And if it doesn't work out with Jasmine, call me because I have some connections here that would be good for a young woman like you." He pulls a business card out of his breast pocket and hands it to her.

"God, Asia, you didn't tell me that you had such a beautiful family. Who'd have thought?" Amber cuts her eyes at me.

Shut the hell up.

"Thank you all so much. And I apologize for interrupting," the little she-devil says as she pushes her chair out and begins to stand. "I guess I better go back over to my seat at the bar." Amber stands amidst many cries of "No, no. Join us."

And I thought that it couldn't get any worse.

Meet the Fam

Am I not destroying my enemies
when I make friends of them?

—Abraham Lincoln

Amber____

By default, the spitting image of Asia introduces me to this very attractive group of people because, as she puts it, "Asia's so rude. Think nobody's taught you nothing."

She beckons me to her with a wave, "Come here, Amber, and meet the fam." She puts her arm around my shoulders and points to herself, "Well, I'm India, Asia's big sister, unfortunately," then she points towards the end of the table. "All the way at the end are my grandparents. Next to them is Uncle Robert and Aunt Helen. That's their son, Jason, and his soon to be wife Layla." That got a chuckle out of the family. Layla frowns at me. I don't know why. "And this handsome fellow is my husband, Ralph," she adds while rubbing his shoulder. "And I guess you know everyone else."

After the introductions, the various conversations resume. I flashback to the first five times that I watched the movie "Soul Food." That movie always makes me wish that I had a family who got together for holidays, a sister to argue with, or a grandmother to mourn.

Asia doesn't know how good she has it.

From what I can tell, the wives are all sitting directly across from their husbands. Since I am on the end, next to Judge Spears, I'm sitting across from Asia's mother who is fascinated by me. Mrs. Spears sits up prim and proper, obviously a product of etiquette school. Every graceful motion she makes, seems effortless.

Her questioning eyes chip at my armor. She delivers every inquiry with immense curiosity in her voice while staring intently in my eyes. Can't tell exactly what she's probing for, but she is *definitely* on the hunt. I know what she shoulda been searching for.

"So Amber, how long will you be in Los Angeles?" Mrs. Spears takes a sip of her coffee without breaking eye contact.

"I head back tomorrow," I poke my lips out into a fake pout. "I'm really going to miss it here. Everything is *sooooo* beautiful."

"Now, now, Chicago has a lot to be admired," she places her coffee on the table. "Although it's an older city, the buildings and structures are historic and some of the best this country has to offer. It's one of the few places that preserve its landmarks."

"That's true," I agree. "Now it just needs to reserve some of this sunshine and import it cross country." We share a laugh together.

Fashion, school, dream vacations and favorite foods are just a few topics that we talk about. After about twenty-five minutes of shooting the breeze with questions which on the surface seem impersonal, but personal at the same time, Mrs. Spears asks, "So Amber, where do your parents live?"

"Uh, Mom, I think Amber's *business* is *Amber's* business," Asia interrupts our conversation until her mother gives her the "shut the hell up or I'ma slap you" look.

"No I don't mind," I smile at Asia who tries to kick me, but misses and kicks the leg of the table instead, causing the table to jerk suddenly. "My parents moved to London after I graduated from high school. My father is a pilot for British Airways and my mother is a flight attendant." This time Asia's pointy toe catches my shin dead on, but I continue, unfazed. "Asia's met my parents."

We both look at Asia who puts on an obviously forced smile, baring no teeth. An inaudible grunt sounding like "Uhn hun," escapes from her lips before me and Mrs. Spears continue talking.

"Because London is their hub, they decided to make it their permanent home. I haven't seen them in years."

"Oh, that's too bad. You must miss them, horribly?" she asks seeming to see the pain in my eyes that I try to shield when talking about my parents or lack thereof. I am glad that only Asia is listening to our conversation.

"So, Mother, how were your crab legs?" Asia asks. I can't tell if she sees my pain as well or if this is another attempt to change the subject. Her mother doesn't look up nor does she answer the question. Her eyes stay glued on me as if I hold the answer for the cure for cancer.

"Yeah, well, I did in the beginning, but now I'm getting used to being alone. I keep myself busy." Then, just to piss Asia off and pay her back for my sore shin, I add, "So, I'm trying to find a surrogate family so that I don't have to spend *all* of my holidays alone."

Mrs. Spears reaches across the table and cups my hands in hers. "Amber, any friend of Asia's is a friend of ours and you can visit us anytime. Do you understand me, Young Lady?"

Asia tries to squash that open invitation and hurriedly jumps in to assure her that, "Mother, you don't have to worry about Amber. I'll make sure that she's occupied on each and every holiday."

Ignored again? Damn girl, you batting a thousand. Mrs. Spears takes out her business card and a pen. After writing a number on the back of the card, she reaches across the table and hands it to me. "This is our home number. My cell is on the front. Call me anytime."

Hanging with them puts me in the mind of what talking to relatives or having a large family must feel like.

After all the hugs and cries of "Hope to see you soon" are given, I walk over to where Mrs. Spears is saying goodbye to India and Ralph. I don't want to leave her. I seldom meet sincere and pleasant people. She puts me at ease. Makes me forget my life.

"Thanks for inviting me to stay, Mrs. Spears," I smile to cover the brewing sadness in my gut and reach out to shake her hand.

"No, please call me Mom," she grabs me and hugs me tight.

Asia stomps her foot so loudly that everyone turns and looks at her.

"Will do, Mom," I say while glaring at Asia over her mother's shoulder. "I'll call you soon."

Clean up
the Forest

You cannot unscramble eggs.

—North American Proverb

*Amber*___

leave Crustacean in a hurry. 12:17. *Shoot, how did I let this happen?* Before I make it to the parking garage, the black Lincoln whips in front of me and the back door opens. I hop in.

"I thought I was going to be late."

"You are." Karob smiles at me and nods. His black, cotton Kufi cap covers most of his hair and forehead.

"How was your night?" I ask him.

"Not as interesting as yours," his accusatory tone is out of character and catches me off guard. "Amber, why don't you leave her alone? What beef do the two of you have?" He looks at me as if he expects an answer.

I slip my dress over my head knowing that that would divert his accusing gaze. He looks out the window. I put my legs in the black, spandex, one-piece body suit that is on the seat between us. I pull the cat suit over my arms and stretch my legs out so that I can zip it.

As we go pass the restaurant, I see Asia and Shaun getting into their car. The tension and frown marks that were gathered around her brow in my company are now completely gone and she looks her normal, happy self.

Maybe I should leave her alone.

In less than ten minutes, we're on Garden Drive in Bel Air. I crack the window and rest the electric scrambling gun on the glass. Every house in this community has between twenty and thirty cameras on the grounds which need to be temporarily disabled while we handle our mission.

The driver turns off the lights as we drive through Bel Air. When he gets close to our stop he slows down and Karob and I jump out of the moving vehicle. After Karob disarms the security system, we scale the rod iron fence, hop down onto the extravagant landscaping, and go in separate directions.

Before I open the door, I put on my Versace glasses. The study is extremely spacious. No furniture except for a large oak desk and two chairs. I place the ultra thin, palm-size monitor on the desk. In the far corner of the room lit only by moonlight, I take a seat and wait. And wait. And wait.

After about an hour, the door opens and Dr. Forest Lewis limps in on his cane, obviously wearing a Christmas gift. Black and red plaid pajama bottoms with matching slippers and a white t-shirt underneath his unbuttoned pajama top. He shuffles to his desk and turns on the lamp before he notices the monitor. I take the remote out of my pocket and push the power button. The monitor pops on.

"What the hell?" he whispers to himself while scratching the Einstein mop on top of his head.

"Does that look familiar?" I ask.

He jumps at the sound of my voice, but looks back down quickly at the screen. He squints at the monitor and yells, "What the hell is going on here?"

"I think I can explain that," I say.

"Well, somebody better get to explaining."

"Your wish is my command," I bow my head respectfully at him. "You see that red dot on your wife's head?"

Dr. Lewis squints at the screen again and then scratches his Einstein fro.

"Well, that's the laser beam of a Beretta. Which is only slightly different from the beam of the .357 Magnum that's on your daughter's head in Phoenix." I click the remote so that it moves to a view of his sleeping daughter. "And your son in Omaha has the top of the line Walther P99." I click the remote again to his son who is pleasuring himself with someone other than his wife with a red dot on the back of his head.

"What's the meaning of all of this?" He grabs his chest and falls back into his chair.

"I think I can answer that as well. See, you've pissed off some people in very high places. In situations like these, paying the piper is as sure as paying taxes."

"Paying by killing my family?"

"You do pay taxes don't you?"

"But why?" Confusion steals the knowledge of the world that his eyes always seem to hold.

"Two words. Panama '98."

Dr. Lewis drops his head into his hands and shakes it slowly from side to side. "So what do they want from me?" He appears to visibly age.

My voice is steady and deliberate as I tell him, "Well, you have two options. Both pretty grim by my estimations, but these are your options nonetheless."

"Anything. What do they want me to do?" He looks up with a glint of hope in his eyes. Dr. Lewis is different from Senator Warren. Yeah, doctors are different from politicians, so I almost feel sorry for him. *Almost.*

"One would be to kill yourself."

"I will do no such thing! Preposterous!"

"I agree," I say while walking slowly towards his desk. "Preposterous," I lift my nose snobbishly in the air. I pick up my monitor, fold it, and slip it back into my pocket.

Dr. Lewis sobs.

"Second option. Refuse, go to jail where you will, by the way, inexplicably hang yourself. A horrible way to die I've been told." I shake my head in feigned sympathy. "And who wouldn't commit suicide after they've lost their entire family in a horrible mass murder that they've so sloppily arranged?"

"Me?! No one will believe that. I love my family."

"Look in your desk at all the evidence that will fall into the hands of the police bit by bit."

Dr. Lewis snatches the desk drawer open and begins looking

slowly, dejectedly through all of the cancelled checks, plane tickets, a pocket calendar with pertinent evidence, and photos of him paying off the hit man.

"But I'm being framed. I have no motive. A good lawyer can beat this."

"Trust me, we have your motive covered as well."

He weeps softly this time.

"Now, that we've gotten that outta the way." I sit on the edge of his desk and point to the bottom drawer. "There's a revolver that you keep in there. You have five minutes from this point to take care of your business or.......or not."

I push the timer on my watch, walk to my spot in the corner, and sit back down in the chair. Before I cross my legs, Dr. Lewis has taken the gun out the drawer, put it in his mouth and, without hesitation, he pulls the trigger. His head falls forward and lands on the desk with a light thud. Gun still in his mouth.

Glad that didn't take long.

"Clean up," I say as I step back out the same way that I had entered.

"In motion," the voice from the microchip in my ear confirms.

Karob and I meet back at the front gate and pass the clean up crew on our way out.

Dark Chocolate Dream

I never met a chocolate I didn't like.

—Deanna Troi

Jazz____

"**Y**ou two! My chambers! Now!" Judge Al Tyler slams his gavel and pushes out of his chair. We follow behind him as he walks slower than a man of fifty should. Sorta like his feet hurt.

As soon as his office door closes, Attorney Smith begins yelling, screaming, rolling her neck, and pointing her fingers. I block out half of her ranting and raving because it ain't gon make a *damn* bit of difference.

"Judge Tyler, she always pulls this mess," she points so hard I'm surprised she doesn't dislocate her shoulder. Dramatics.

She now counts off on her fingers, "She claimed that someone mailed her evidence on the Pemsco Case, the Levee Case, the Stymied Case, and the VanCo Case."

Ooops, she ran outta fingers.

"And you're claiming that they didn't? So I'm a liar now, huh? You think I'd risk being disbarred? For what?" I ask with an innocent look on my face before I turn to face Judge Tyler. "Your Honor, people get anonymous tips all the time. I don't understand why Attorney Smith acts like this is so weird."

"It is weird when it happens to the same person *all* the time. What kinda mess is that?"

"It's weird that you think that it's okay to give hysterectomies to elderly women in nursing homes just to 'keep down confusion.' Your grandmother must be very proud."

"I've heard enough from the two of you. This bickering has to stop. Today! You will not make a mockery of my courtroom!" He looks at the both of us, but stares at me a little longer. "Attorney Livingston, I will allow the admission of this evidence, but if I suspect that there was any foul play involved in getting these documents, I'll hold you in contempt."

Contempt is for simps. "Yes Your Honor, you don't have to worry about that." *I don't get caught.*

We both leave his office. Attorney Smith stands in front of me outside the chambers, "You may have fooled the judge, but I'm on to you. You betta watch yo' back from here on out." She bumps my shoulder as she walks away.

Okay, she has one more time to do that and I'ma break her lil' ass in half. Don't get it twisted. My daddy ain't raise no punk.

I stand in the courthouse lobby dreading stepping one foot into the half foot that has fallen in the three hours that I have been inside. Yeah, I like the snow, but this is crazy. The blustery wind does nothing but add fuel to the fire by lifting already settled snow off the ground to engage in a territorial battle with the subzero temperatures.

I should have done this earlier.

I pull my hat down over my eyebrows and tie my scarf around my mouth and nose so that only the whites of my eyes are showing. My cotton gloves are snuggly on for insulation before I put my hands into my more stylish leather gloves. For the final coat of armor, I pull my hood over my head.

Nothing that I have on is able to resist the cutting wind. I pick my angle like many of the other daredevils who had come out before me. By the time I make it to Marshall Fields, I am mad, cold, and evil. I rush into the store in between droves of people looking for after Christmas shopping sales. My desire is to get in and out of that store quickly, but my defrost time may be an hour. *Shoot, I don't think I can feel my toes.*

The eight-story department store is festively decorated. Shoppers are greeted by a fifty-foot frosted Christmas tree with ornaments from over a hundred countries and topped with the traditional star. The little drummer boy is leading a band in the fragrance department while the shepherds surround a newborn baby in a manger by the jewelry section. I weave in and out of the compulsive shoppers. As soon as I finish at the gift wrapping station, I call Chase.

"Baby, I'm hopping in a cab now headed home."

"You may want to take the Metra 'cuz the Dan Ryan is mess.

You know how everyone acts like they ain't never drove in the snow?"

"Ooh, I'm getting a headache just thinking about it, but it's too cold to wait on the L-platform for a train in this weather. I opt to save my extremities and catch a cab."

"Yeah, you may be right. Did you get the gifts?"

"I'm leaving Marshall Fields as we speak. I feel like I've just violated Kuumba though. There is nothing creative in buying somebody something that is made in a range of sizes, colors, and is on sale because of overstock and fourth quarter profit margins."

"I know baby. But this is the first time that we didn't make the gifts for Kwanzaa and I'm sure your parents will understand that we both were a little busy this year."

"Yeah, well I hope so," I say as I flag down a cab. "And it was crowded in there. If I had a gun I would have shot myself. Or somebody else. I could've gone postal up in there."

"Well, I'm glad you didn't," he laughs because he evidently thinks I am joking.

"Alright Chase, I'll be there in twenty minutes."

"See you when you get here."

An hour and fifteen gruesome minutes later, after avoiding four head on collisions and two possible ditch visits, I walk into our ranch-style home. I immediately begin shedding the insufficient layers of protection and drop them on the floor, next to my bags. I head straight for the bedroom in hopes of sprawling across our king-size pillow top mattress and tucking myself underneath the goose down comforter.

Chase is closing the last of four suitcases on our bed. "Baby, what's going on? You're not leaving me already are you?" I choke out as much of a laugh as I can muster while rubbing my hands together to warm them.

Chase walks towards the armoire and picks up the red envelope with a red satin bow placed decoratively on top. "I figured for Imani this year, we could have faith in the airline." He hands me the envelope and smiles, showing the gap that hooked me all those years ago. Sexy.

For a moment, I'm thirteen again and getting my first pair of 14k gold hoops from my father. I take a deep breath and then slowly open the envelope. Inside are two tickets to Hawaii.

Shoot! And I only bought him a few pair of pants, some shirts, and underwear. I have to get better at this gift buying thing.

"Ooh Chase. You are absolutely the best guy a girl could ever want." I jump into his arms and we both fall on the bed. Our lips meet in a hot, wet union. "How could you have known that I always wanted to take my mother to Hawaii?"

He looks at me sideways, "Your mother?" and then he begins tickling me. "I got your mother."

"Okay, okay, I was just joking." I yell between painful laughs while trying to wiggle away from his playful fingers.

"Are you sure 'cuz I can do this all night?" He tickles me until I roll off the bed and run out of the room. The living room offers no refuge.

By the couch, he tortures me relentlessly. I have to use the only weapon I have. I pull his Reebok jogging pants down with one hand while I grab Rambo with the other hand. It's been called "Rambo" since the first time it broke my back, knocked me out, and left me walking bowlegged for a week. I fall to my knees, caress his muscular thighs, and begin pleasuring my husband.

I grab his head and slip Rambo into my mouth, *"Mmm,* do you believe me now?"

"Uh, uh, not yet," he rests his hands on the top of my head. "What you gon' do to convince me?"

I lick and suck Rambo gently at first trying to pace myself. My tongue circles round and round and round until finally I take his whole shaft in my mouth, opening my mouth wide when going down and closing my lips tightly around it when coming back up.

"Oh shit, Baby. That feels good."

I increase the pace and tighten my mouth more around him. He moans with pleasure. I moan with him and go faster and faster until he pulls away in ecstasy.

"You believe me now?" I smile as he falls back on the couch.

I hop up and go get a wet face cloth. When I come back with the warm towel, Chase's eyes are closed, his chest is moving up and down slowly, and I know that snoring is the final stage of this episode.

I stare at my Hershey-colored dark chocolate dream with black wavy hair. His thin-line sideburns cascade down to meet his neatly trimmed goatee. And those lips. *Damn, how did I get so lucky?* He wakes up when the warm towel touches him.

"Thanks, Jazzy. You're the best girl a guy could ever want."

I take both his hands, help him off the couch, and pull up his sweats that are around his ankles. He wraps his arms around my neck and kisses me on the forehead.

"So when are we leaving?" In all the excitement, I forgot to look at the ticket.

Chase now falls to his knees in front of me. He slowly unbuttons my pants. "Right after," he kisses and licks my belly button, "we have dinner," he takes off my pants, "at your," he pulls my thongs down with his teeth, "parent's house," he gently lays me on the couch, "tomorrow." He spreads my legs and buries his face between them. Taking as much care with me as I had with him.

God, I love chocolate.

Khriswanzaa

One ever feels his twoness-an American, a
Negro; two souls, two thoughts, two un-
reconciled strivings; two warring ideals
in one dark body, whose dogged strength
alone keeps it from being torn asunder.
                                    —W.E.B. DuBois

Jazz____

"I see why they win every year," Chase says as we turn onto my
parent's block. In Beverly, the residents compete in the city-
wide Christmas decoration contest. My parent's block has won
three years in a row.

"Wow, look at that one." I point to a house that is designed to look
like a gingerbread house with candy canes lit up all around. Plastic
figures sit on the lawn around a fireplace mechanically opening gifts.
I could see traces of the fake snow peeping from underneath the real
thing. Each house has a life size glow Santa in the yard.

"They really did the thang this year," Chase points as we pass a three home exhibit with Rudolph the red nose reindeer. The first house has Rudolph on the ground ready for take off. The second house has the reindeer suspended from a tree headed for their Christmas Eve journey. And the third house has them on top of the roof with Santa's hat sticking out of the chimney.

As soon as we walk in, I smell Momma's lamb chops. The family's secret recipe that she's been using to marinate the sauce makes Karamu dinner the best. "This Christmas" by Donny Hathaway that is spinning at 45 rpm's on the antique record player, is letting us know that our Kwanzaa slash Christmas celebration is beginning. Chase likes to jokingly call it "Khriswanzaa," but we'd never say it in front of my mother.

"Momma, we're here," I yell.

Chase heads straight for the dining room table to see what dish he can pick in without anyone noticing.

The mkeka mat is in the middle of the table with a kinara centerpiece holding seven candles, three red, one black, and three green. This candelabrum holds one candle representing each of the seven days of Kwanzaa. Only one is not lit today and that's the green candle that my parents will light tomorrow when they have their private dinner date in celebration of unity.

Also, on the mkeka are two ears of corn, a fruit basket, and a unity cup. The room is decorated with red, black, and green balloons, streamers, and clothes. There are many African dishes on the table, but Chase goes straight for Momma's homemade dinner rolls.

I head to the kitchen. I feel like I am at a railroad crossing so I stop, look, and listen to make sure my mother isn't around. I peek into all the pots, pans, and casserole dishes. If she knew that

I was about to sample her collard greens, she would have my neck in the pot instead of the smoked turkey.

As I'm just about to put my fork back in the pot, Momma walks in. "Chile, what you doing over there?"

I whip around trying to hide my fork, looking like a deer caught in the headlights. *How is it that a 300 pound woman can walk up and not be heard?*

I just shrug my shoulders and laugh. "Hey, Ma. How long have you been standing there?" I discreetly slip the fork in the sink.

"Long enough to know I need to whip your behind 'bout being over my pots. Now get over here and give your momma a hug."

Her red Liz Claiborne pants suit with a brown and burgundy Kente clothe draped over her left shoulder announces that she's done cooking and ready for company. I brace myself for the bear hugs that Momma always gives. She has the bosom of an old church mother. Carolina Herrera and baby powder fill my nostrils as I linger in that familiar place between my mother's mountains.

"Where's Daddy?"

"He's in his library. Asked not to be disturbed until dinnertime."

I want to go in to see him but no one disturbs Daddy when he's in his library. Sometimes he'll call Chase in there. I guess for some type of male bonding thing. But nobody else.

"Where's Lonnie?"

Momma rolls her eyes. "You know where he is."

The sound of PlayStation and laughter linger outside the den. "Hey lil' brother," I say unable to keep the holiday spirit in my voice when I walk in on my brother, Lonnie, lying comfortably with his head on John's lap.

Lonnie and John have been friends since little league. Being the sons of best friends and next door neighbors kept Lonnie and John in the same house, and bed, more often than they should have been, in my estimation. Lonnie gets off the couch and comes over to hug me.

The first time I had noticed that anything was wrong was when Lonnie was fourteen and I was seventeen. I had to wake them up on this particular day because my mother had the flu. When I walked into the room, the alarm clock was blaring. And, although there were twin beds in the room, they were asleep in the same bed together, with Lonnie curled up behind John. All up on his ass. Neither of them had on shirts and the room had a funny smell. Not just the "stinky boy room" smell as me and all my friends who had brothers call it, but something extra.

"Jasmine, what took you so long? I've been waiting to beat your ass in this new NCAA Dynasty," he holds up his sagging, oversized G-Unit jeans with one hand.

I hold up one finger and move it from side to side, "Not in this time, dimension, or on this planet will you ever beat me at any football game, virtual or otherwise."

"Ooooh, sounds like a challenge to me," John says as he laughs into a balled up fist.

"Only because this is sixth day of Kwanzaa and I'm supposed to be focusing on my creative side, I will have to defer the offer and remind you of who's the baddest in *this* house another day." *Especially since there was no creativity involved in the gifts that I'm giving.*

Lonnie cocks his head to the side as if doubting my abilities. "Sounds like an educated way of copping out to me."

"Speaking of copping out, are you two out of the closet now?"

The two of them look at each other in disbelief. "Huh?" I ask looking from one muscular, broad chest man to another. "Because from this vantage point, you two can join in the parade right behind that Simmons guy."

"See, there you go. You know we ain't gay," Lonnie says while John just shakes his head in disgust before returning to the video game. "We both got girlfriends and you know it."

"How would I know that with you all up in his lap like a happy toy poodle? All laid up in Momma's house like this is the Zanzibar Motel. Yo' ass is nasty."

Chase walks in taking a bite off of what is probably his third homemade dinner rolls. "What's going on?" He looks from me to Lonnie then to John searching for answers. When there is no response, he says, "Babe, you're not in here messing with them again, are you?"

I roll my eyes at him and walk out of the room. If someone had struck a match the house would have went kaboom because I was fuming.

I go straight to my mother that day, just as I had done all those years ago and say the exact same thing, "Momma them boys ain't right."

Momma places the lamb roast in the center of the dining room table so that it is surrounded by the collard greens, cabbage, plantains in coconut milk, jollof rice, mashed potatoes, sweet potatoes, curry eggplant, turkey and dressing, and cranberry sauce. She tries to put on her poker face when she says, "Jaybird, it's all in your head," then she lowers her eyes and walks back into the kitchen to get the rest of the Khriswanzaa dinner.

Daisies
on the Floor

Fuck tha police coming straight from the
underground. Young nigga got it bad
cuz I'm brown.

—NWA

Jazz_____

I can get used to this. The first class seats are comfortable and roomy. Friendly and personable flight attendants are accessible. The ride even seems smoother in first class. No turbulence at all.

But there's something about being trapped in an area that if you could escape you'd still be 40,000 feet away from civilization that makes me uneasy. I couldn't sleep the entire ten hour flight to Hawaii.

Chase waits for our bags, while I'm in the limo unable to keep my eyes open another minute. I didn't even hear him get in the limo and don't awake until we pull in front of Ka'anapali Beach Resort in Maui. When we make it to our suite, I lie across the king-size bed in all my clothes and go back to sleep.

I don't know how long I'm asleep before I wake up to the familiar voice of Tamaran Hall, a news anchor from Chicago. "They get Fox News Chicago in Hawaii?" I ask while rubbing my eyes.

"Yeah, this hotel has an awesome satellite dish. It gets the local channels in London. I just finished watching the London Towers beat Maccabi Tel Aviv in the basketball playoffs," Chase says smiling.

"And that makes you smile? Gross." I frown at him causing him to pick up a pillow and throw it at me allowing me to see all the muscles in his arms and back thanks to the wife beater he's wearing. *Mmm, throw something else at me with yo' fine ass.*

"And this just across the wires," Tamaran Hall is saying, "Two Chicago police officers have disappeared while on duty. Officer David Washington is a twenty-three year veteran with the Chicago Police Department, and Officer Juan Menendez has been with the force for seventeen years. Their squad car was found earlier today in an area outside of their district. Officials are trying to figure out how it got there. Several people in the neighborhood have been questioned, but so far the whereabouts of the officers are still unknown. Although there is no sign of force or struggle, foul play is suspected. We will bring you more details as they become available."

"What is wrong with people today?" I ask in disbelief. "The police are the good guys. The ones out there protecting us from harm and danger."

"They're not all good all the time, Jazzy."

"Yeah, but who is? They put their lives on the line everyday. Police are the reason why any of us get to step out our front doors without being clocked over the head." I stand up and put one hand on my hip and point to the TV. "These people think it's their God-given right to commit crimes and not pay for it."

Chase walks over to his suitcase and begins feverishly looking for something. Patting his Enyce jean pockets, jacket pocket, carryon luggage.

"And Chase, you have to admit that the police department's gotten better in the last five or ten years. Daley has really cleaned it up."

"Yeah, it's definitely been cleaned up, but I don't know how much Daley had to do with it."

Chase likes to shock me with his cynical side every now and then, but he really has zero interest in politics or current events. I have to make him watch the news. But regardless, he knows good and well that Daley cleaned up the police department.

I look back at the television as the field reporter questions one neighborhood resident, "I ain't seen nothing," a thirty something, unintelligible, unkempt Black man with a missing tooth was saying while several young kids in the background are jumping up and down, making funny faces at the camera. Then using the triple negative for effect he says, "As a matter of fact, ain't nobody 'round here seen nothing," which generates nods and affirmations from the people behind him.

I shake my head at the display of ignorance. "They have this code of silence thing that puts a huge divide between them and the law. They don't even know that they're hurting themselves. 'Ain't nobody seen nothing.' Pitiful. Just pitiful."

"Yeah yeah, I know. Have you seen my cell phone?"

"It's in my purse," I point in the direction of my purse without looking up from the television. "Remember I had to use it during our layover in New Mexico because my phone wasn't getting reception around those mountains."

Chase takes out his phone. "I need to make a quick phone call." He kisses me on the forehead trying to snap me out of the bad mood that the newscast has put me in. "It shouldn't take long. I've showered. Why don't you hop in the shower so that we can go out and have some dinner," he heads toward the balcony to make his phone call.

"Are you okay? You seem a little.....something. I don't know," I turn off the television.

"Just a little jet lag, I think. I'll be alright tomorrow," he closes the balcony door behind him.

Jet lag? He never gets jet lag. I go to the bathroom. The jacuzzi looks so inviting, but I decide to wait until we finish dinner before I indulge. Inside the huge bathroom, there are two vanity mirrors on opposite sides and two doors. I open the first door, but that room only has a bidet and the toilet. The second room has another toilet with a full bath and shower.

I shower quickly and then peek out the bathroom to see if Chase is impatiently waiting for me. He is still on the phone, talking forcefully with his hands. The only time he's done that lately is when he's talking about work.

Not on my vacation, he's not.

I walk towards the door, then I realize I can't rush him off the phone since I'm not dressed. I put on my white sundress with the yellow daisies all over it and pin my hair up off my neck.

By the time I finish with all that, Chase is done with his phone call.

"Baby, you look absolutely astonishing," he walks over and looks me intensely in the eyes. "I don't know if you realize how much I adore you."

I look at my watch. "I can't tell. I've been feeling neglected for about sixteen minutes."

"I think I can fix that." He kisses me gently on my forehead, cheeks and then on my lips. He lifts me up and puts me on the bed. My yellow daisies are on the floor.

What's the Rush

Patience is a virtue.
—African Proverb

Chase_____

I glare at the UPS man who is an hour late. "Okay, you got one, two, three, four, five packages and you say they all going t' the same place?"

"Yeah, same address."

"COD?"

"Yeah, he'll pay for it when it's delivered," I answer in a calm voice since one of my New Year's resolutions is to control my temper and exercise patience.

"And they know this?" he asks with skepticism in his voice and across his brow.

I just look at him because he has already been here fifteen minutes longer than necessary and if I say anything I chance messing up my resolution. And it's only February.

"Hey man, we gotta ask. You 'on know how many COD's get returned each day. I'm just doing my job."

"Yeah, I know. Just doing your job. Is that all?"

"Yeah, just sign here so that you can get a receipt of delivery and I'll give you the paper with your tracking number on it because with $50,000 in insurance, you want to make sure you can find this sucker."

He holds the electronic signature box for me to sign and then prints out the receipt with my tracking number.

God, what a weekend. Ain't enough hours in the day to fill all the requests that I get around Valentine's Day. Jazz usually comes home early this time of the year to make sure I eat because I will go all day without as much as a cracker. She can't do it this year because of the new firm and the amount of business coming in.

I get off the sofa and go to the kitchen to grab my fourth cup of coffee before I head back to my studio.

The message waiting button is flashing on my answering machine. I press it. Beep. "Chaaaassse, pick up if you're there. It's wifey. Okay well, call me when you get a chance. Love you. Don't work too hard."

Impossible, I think.

Beep. "Chay Chay, this is me, Malik. I need to talk to you." *What's wrong now?* "Make sure you call me when you get this message. You got the number." Beep.

I push the speed dial button labeled, "Love," and wait for her to answer. There is no greeting or salutation when she answers the phone, "You must be extremely busy if you haven't called me back in three hours."

"Yeah. I got caught up in trying to get these orders complete before Saturday. What's up, Babe?"

"I just had to call and tell you that you were right."

"About what?" I ask.

"Remember those two officers, uh.. what's their names?" I hear Jazz shuffling through some papers. "Officer David Washington and Officer Juan Menendez. You know, the two who are missing that they still haven't found yet?"

"Yeah?"

"Turns out that their hands were a little dirty. The reason it's taking them so long to get any leads on what could have happened to them is because they've created so many enemies. Taking pay-offs, stealing drugs, extortion. The list goes on and on."

"Really?"

"And guess what else? They're the ones investigating the little white girl who was killed around your mother's house. And they're not even assigned to that area."

"Well, that's interesting."

"Interesting! Is that all you can say? Don't you smell that?"

"Smell what?"

"Fish, baby, fish. If it looks like a fish and smells like a fish, my guess is that it's probably fish."

"Jazzy, maybe you should—"

She covers up the receiver, but I can still hear a muffled, "Yes, yes. I'm on my way." She comes back to the phone and says, "Sorry Baby, I have to get to this meeting. I'll finish telling you everything when I see you tonight. Love you," she hangs up the phone.

I pull the phone away from my ear and look at it. Talking about I'm busy? She's the one too busy to begin or end a phone call. I hang up the phone and find myself pacing the floor.

That explains why the police were swarming the neighborhood that night and weeks after Malik fired all of them shots. Anytime something happens to a white person, the police department pulls out all the stops. But when that Black girl in Englewood was raped and killed, all they could do was blame a seven and eight year old boy for the crime.

I dial Malik's cell phone in L.A. He picks up on the first ring, "Why you just calling me back?"

What happened to Hi? How you doing? What's the damn rush?

"Been busy. Whatcha need?"

"I'll be graduating from rehab in three weeks. I can't wait to be out in the real world."

"I bet. Six months is a long time. Momma's gon' be so happy," I try not to get too emotional. Although I'm excited about having my brother back to normal, he's let me down too many times.

"And you know dem classes I've been takin' on da' net?"

"Yeah, the classes to become an electrical engineer," I can remember like it was yesterday that I had to pick up Malik from Northern Illinois University during his junior year because he had got hold to some bad drugs and was running around naked outside of Altgeld Hall. Messing up his full scholarship for engineering. Ain't been back since.

"The rehab got it set up so that I can start going to classes as soon as I'm released even if it is the middle of the semester."

"Good. You keep your head focused on that and I'll handle it down here in the trenches. Plus, I need to find out about the little dead girl."

"What dead girl?"

I fill Malik in on the details of what Jazz had just told me. He goes from zero to ten in a split second when he finds out that this dead girl is white. He understands the gravity of the situation.

"This ain't gon' be over 'til they string up some nigga. Whether he guilty or not."

I hate it when he uses the "N" word. But I can only focus on one character flaw at a time.

"And if Jazz got anything to do with it, she gon' find out the truth," he says as my doorbell rings.

"Malik, somebody's at my door. Gotta go. I'll talk to you next week, but don't sweat it yet. It may be nothing," I lie as I let Malik go and rush to the front door.

Grab Yo' Shit

One man cannot hold another man
down in a ditch without remaining
down in there with him.

—Booker T. Washington

Chase_____

I open the door and Shaun rushes in talking a mile a minute. "Now it's still not too late for you to go to Amsterdam with me, C-Dog. It's gon' be hot." He puts his hands up like he's framing a portrait. "Picture this. I've reserved a room at the Flying Pig."

"The Flying Pig?! But you said....."

"I know...I know. I said that we would be staying at the Barbizon Palace, but this hostel is a four star and it's downtown Amsterdam where all the happenings are. Trust me on this, Chase. The most beautiful women in the world will be there. College girls on spring break. Everything." He's still looking into his imaginary picture frame and smiling at the images inside of there.

"Jazz ain't not going for it. I didn't even mention it to her."

"Dog, who grabs dick and scratches balls in this family? You or Jasmine?"

I look at Shaun and shake my head. *What prehistoric world is he living in?*

"I'm serious. I ain't seen you grab your dick since high school when you were a lil' gang banger. That's when you was a real man." He laughs. "Go ahead. I bet you're scared to grab your dick." He crosses his arms and smirks at me. "What? Let me guess." He puts his hands on his hips and tries to take his tenor to soprano when he says, "Jasmine say you can't grab yo' dick no mo'?"

"Man, I've had a long day. I ain't got time for this."

I walk towards the kitchen and Shaun jumps in front of me. He puts his arms straight out in front of him and walks like a zombie while talking in a monotone voice, "Jazz says me no touch dick. No touch dick." He grabs me by the shoulders with his zombie hands.

"Man, get away from me," I laugh and push him off me.

"C-Dog, really, I think Jasmine has you thinking that what's between your legs is her dick and not yours. Grab yo' shit to let her know it ain't true." He looks at me and waits. "Go ahead."

Just to shut him up, I reach down and grab my dick then let it go.

"What the hell was that? Did it burn your hand or something?" He shakes his hand like he touched a hot stove. "Ouch!"

"Shaun, you know you crazy?"

"Me?" He points to himself before pointing at me. "You the man without a dick. If that ain't some crazy shit then I don't know what is."

I start sorting through all the tracking receipts that I've collected from UPS today hoping that maybe he would think that I'm busy and leave.

"See Dog, when we get older and more mature, we lose some of our manhood. I just want to bring some of that back. Now, do like this." Shaun grabs between his legs, jerks his stuff around in his hand, and then just holds his hand there. He strolls across the room with an exaggerated strut and still does not remove his hand from his dick.

Sometimes I swear I think he's high on something.

"Shaun, none of this is gonna change the fact of the matter. I can't go. I don't want to cheat on my wife with a bunch of beautiful women. I *already have* a beautiful woman to make love to."

"Then you *already know* how good it is. So what's the problem?" he extends his hands like he's doing an altar call.

"What the *hell* is your fascination with fucking around on your wife? Asia is wonderful, thoughtful, kind, beautiful, and loves your dirty drawers. Which confuses the hell outta me."

"Asia loves my money."

"You know that ain't true. Asia has her own money."

"Don't try to get off the subject. Are you going or not? Be a man. Grab your balls." Shaun smiles and waits for a response. "I'll make it worth your while."

"If I come, it'll only be for a couple days, not a couple weeks. And I ain't getting caught up in none of yo' bullshit either. No strip clubs, no blow jobs, no orgies, no ménage a trois. Nothing. Got it?"

"Chase, Chase, Chase. Ménage a trois?" he shakes his head in shear disbelief. "Must I teach you *everything?* That term ain't been used since Mother Teresa was doing it. Now, it's called double dippin'." He dips his voice and body for emphasis.

"Double *damn* dippin'?" I cock my head. "And Mother Teresa was doing it, huh?" Now it's my turn to shake my head in disbelief. "Outta all the morons in high school that I coulda hooked up with and kept for the long haul, you was the best that I could do. What does that say about me?"

"See, think of it like this." Shaun puts up his picture frame hands again like my question wasn't legitimate. "You go to Baskin Robbins for some ice cream, right. And you're tempted by *aaalllll* your options. But being the conservative guy that you are, you decide not to be greedy. 'Two scoops please,' you say to the sexy cashier with the big butt.

"Now you licking say....the Caramel Mocha." He grabs a paint brush off the table and holds it up to his mouth and sticks his tongue out like he's licking it.

"But yo' second scoop, which is French Vanilla, is calling yo' name." He looks at the paint brush like it's Halle Berry on a stick and licks again. "Mmm, mmm. Damn that tastes good." He shivers like he can taste the goodness and feel the coldness in his bones.

"So instead of finishing off the Caramel Mocha 'cuz it's on top, you lick that French Vanilla down *reaaalll* good. Now you got them both on yo' tongue and yo' chin and you realize that they taste *sooooo* much better together that you'll *never* go back to having just one flavor. Never, ever, *ever* again in life. Double dippin'. That's called living my brotha'. Believe me, I know."

"Shaun?"

"Yeah?"

"Get cho' crazy ass outta my house. I got work to do." I walk to the door and stifle a laugh because I know that that would only encourage him to come up with some mo' ole crazy shit.

"Don't trip. I gotta go anyway. You ain't the only one got work to do." He flicks his collar like he's one cool cat. "Brotha' got a very important meeting with a red mini skirt and her best friend. Double the pleasure." He walks out the door and then turns back with seriousness in his eyes and asks, "But in my absence, can you do one thing for me?"

"What is it now, Shaun?"

"Practice grabbing yo' dick." He reaches down and grabs his shit again. "I'm telling you, it's therapeutic. It'll help you keep your sanity." He laughs all the way to his car.

Different Angles

Life's battles don't always go to the stronger or faster man. But sooner or later, the man who wins is the man who thinks he can.

—Unknown

Jazz

"On the case of Elizabeth Brown versus Cherish Nursing Home, we find the defendant liable for negligence and abuse and award the plaintiff a sum of $14.3 million." Judge Tyler slams his gavel.

Mrs. Brown sits there unaffected by the verdict. She's in her final stage of Alzheimer. I bend down and hug her anyway. At ninety-eight, she has no living relatives. Everyone died before her. So there's no one to enjoy the money, but it doesn't matter. It's not about that. It's about sending a message out there to anyone who thinks they can get away with hurting the elderly. I will work pro bono to take these cases.

Attorney Smith walks over to me and I hold my hand out to shake on a good fight. She looks down at my hand like she could spit on it.

Is the $14 mil coming outta your bank account?

"I will be filing an appeal," she adjusts the strap to the briefcase on her shoulder.

I want to ask on what grounds, but I don't because all my bases are covered.

"Spin your wheels if you must, just don't bump into me again," I warn her because I've been feeling like slapping somebody lately. Might as well be her.

She balls up her fist and stomps to the courtroom exit.

Accepting the fact that you're a loser on a losing team may help with your anger management issues, I think as she forcefully pushes the courtroom doors open.

Back at the office our meeting has begun. I take a seat at the table and give Amber thumbs up so that she knows I won the case. She smiles and gives me double thumbs.

"Are we equipped to take on the City of Harvey and the Chicago Police Department in the same month?" Mitch asks. "Both of these cases will be high profile."

"And the City will bring in the best lawyers from around the country," Tom closes the file and pushes it to the center of the table.

"Which only means that we have to be better than the best," I jump in. *I know I'm better than the best,* I think to myself, feeling a little cocky after my latest conquest. "If they bring in some big time lawyers, we know how to contract out their competition if we have to."

"How are we going to divide the cases up?" John asks. "Me and Tom can do the police department scandal and Mitch and Jasmine can do the manipulative bidding for public procurement case."

"Actually, I think we all should work both cases," I suggest.

John shakes his head in protest. "Nobody does that. That would be too much work and our focus would be split, weakening both of our cases."

"Our focus may be split, but our efforts will be compiled," I argue. "See, what we could do is have two round table meetings daily to discuss our progress. The first one will be at seven. This one will recap the day before and be our planning meeting for the day. The second meeting will be after lunch. We'll give each other an update of what we've accomplished thus far."

"Lunch? Who gets to eat lunch around here?" Tom lightens the mood and we laugh.

"No, but seriously, how is this better than just splitting the cases up?" Mitch is not convinced and wants to know.

"Well for both of these cases we're going to be going up against teams of six to eight attorneys," I say pointing out at the skyline. "Not because the city is show boating, but because you need that much manpower to do one of these cases. Now if we're planning on winning these cases or at least not being slaughtered, we're going to have to take a different approach. Small firms don't have the luxury afforded to big firms."

"I think she may be right," Tom concedes. "When the four of us are together, we are dynamic. Different angles, scenarios, and tactics are thrown on the table and it always helps to hear so many different sides to an argument. I say we do it."

"I'm still not buying it. It sounds like a recipe for disaster to me." Mitch says.

"Well let's try it for a month," I compromise. "After our morning round table, we'll dedicate the first five hours to the police department and the second five hours to the bidding fiasco. That way in the morning, if I come to ask a question about the police department, you'll have your information available and fresh because we have certain hours that we do certain things. We can come up with assignments tomorrow."

Three hours later, I'm finally back in my office and I still haven't done the most important thing of the day. I push the intercom button.

"Yes, Attorney Livingston?"

"Ms. Cherrington, can you come in here for a sec?"

Amber sashays in with her princess walk and glamour girl smile to match. "Yes, Attorney Livingston. What can I get for you?"

"Amber, I have a dilemma."

"Finally. A dilemma." She folds her hands in prayer, looks up and mouths the words thank you.

I laugh at her melodramatics. No matter how much work I give her, she finishes quickly and always seems like it's not quite exciting enough.

"Valentine's Day is coming up and I haven't gotten Chase anything. I can't even think of anything to get him. I need some suggestions."

Amber starts rattling off suggestions with the enthusiasm that only a twenty-something year old could. It's good to have this energy around the office. She offers a different perspective, another slant. When Shaun called a month back and asked if I could use a paralegal, I was skeptical. The last time I did someone a hiring favor, it backfired on me.

But not with Amber. Youthful and passionate, without being immature puts her at the top of the game. Best of all, she's sharp and willing to learn.

I had been trying for years to convince Rebecca to retake the Bar. Amber talked to her for thirty minutes and voila, done. Rebecca had planned to train Amber for a couple of weeks, but it only took a few days.

Amber's so good that I'm willing to foot the bill for law school in exchange for her working for the firm for the five years following her graduation. I haven't told her yet. I'm just waiting to see how she does on the LSAT next month.

"How could he not be into clothes?" Amber squeals. "Oh my God, I would *absolutely* die, if I didn't have my Prada shoes and matching belt blending with my Prada skirt suit." Amber points at all of the items that she is wearing that she thinks she would *absolutely* die without.

"Trust me, Amber. He's an artist. I have a hard enough time trying to get him to wear matching socks."

"He looks okay every time I see him."

"That's because I lay his clothes out every night."

"Well, I'm all out of suggestions." Amber throws her hands up in the air and lets them fall noisily onto her lap. "Does he drink beer?"

"Didn't you know? That's the one irreversible flaw of the

entire male species—their inability to live without beer."

"That's it then. There is a beer of the month club where they deliver a different case of foreign beer every month."

"No way! When did they start that?"

"It's been around for years. They have a club for everything. Wine of the month, plants, cakes, pizza, chips. Anything you can think of. I think they will send him twelve beers each month."

"Perfect. That's the perfect gift for any man. I can give him that every year and he'd be happy." I go into my wallet and pass her my credit card.

"Amber, you are a lifesaver. A real lifesaver."

"Sssh, I am a lifesaver, but don't tell anybody or I may have to kill you," she laughs and leaves my office.

Sashay, sashay.

Robes
with Hearts

True love comes quietly, without banners or
flashing lights. If you hear bells, get your
ears checked.

—Erich Segal

Jazz____

Of course when I wake up that Saturday on Valentine's Day,
Chase is not in the bed. I can hear him clanking around in
the kitchen and sweet cinnamon fills my nostrils. I go to the bathroom to take my shower and the tub is prepared with warm water
and rose petals. Because my skin feels smooth and silky within
minutes, I can tell that he had added a couple of drops of my Rosa
damascena, the rose oil that Asia bought for me when she went to
Bulgaria a few years back.

I remember the first time Chase and I celebrated Valentine's Day together. Things had progressed rapidly after I met him at Daddy's dojo. We had only known each other, couldn't even call it dating at that point, for two and a half months. Chase had a dozen Casablanca lilies delivered to my office, two at a time, for the first six hours with sweet notes from a secret admirer. A box of my favorite candy, white chocolate toffee, spelling out my name was delivered in the seventh hour. And then he revealed his identity with a card letting me know that a chauffer would be picking me up from work in a half hour. Attached to that card was the poem that is taped on the bathroom mirror.

Roses are red.

Violets are blue.

I would be delighted

if I could spend Valentine's Day with you.

Truly,

Chase

That was delivered last. When I was dropped off at the restaurant, I felt like a teenager with a new fresh puppy love. Puppy love is the best. So every year since our first, he tries to keep up the tradition. He loves Valentine's Day.

It's hard to pull myself out of the tub, but since I know he is cooking breakfast, I force myself. The dining room table is adorned with a white tablecloth, red and yellow rose petals scattered on top and rose-scented candles burning.

When he sees me, he grabs the remote to the CD player and presses play. I stand at the dining room entrance waiting for Prince's "When 2 R in Love" to come on. That's our Valentine's Day theme song.

He takes my hand, pulls me into his arms, and we begin slow dancing as he sings in my ear along with Prince. "When 2 R in love, they whisper secrets only 2 can hear. When 2 R in love." I smile the entire time he's singing to me, on key, off key, in between keys. It all sounds good to me.

When the song goes off, he gives me a long sensuous kiss before walking me over to the table.

"How was your bath?" he pulls my chair out.

"Great. Thanks baby," I smile up at him and he kisses me again.

The oven alarm rings, "Your timing is superb, Madame. Your food will be out momentarily," Chase says in his best Dutch accent.

He comes back and puts the German apple pancake in front of me. The second trip is a tray with the rest of the meal which includes eggs, bacon, sliced fruit and orange juice.

We talk and eat slowly. Every story told ends in laughter. And although I'm eating the biggest pancake in the world, served on a platter, I feel ten pounds lighter. Laughter is truly medicinal.

As soon as I swallow my last bite of pancake, Chase says, "I need you to look behind you."

"Look behind me?"

"Yeah, just look behind you," his grin turns into a full-blown smile now.

I turn around and there is a huge painting of the two of us. We look to be about fifty-five years old in this age-progressed painting. I'm sitting on the sofa that we got last year, but which looks worn and comfortable in the painting. I'm reading a Dr. Seuss book to a two or three year old little girl who is propped up on my lap. And Chase is tickling a boy who is a few years older. Our grandkids. In the background I can see a young woman with both of our features, obviously our daughter holding hands with her husband.

I can't speak. *Amazing,* I think as the tears roll down my cheeks.

I pull out his card for the Beer of the Month Club. "I have to get better at this gift buying thing." The tears continue to roll.

"Jazz, you *are* my gift." He reaches out, takes my hand, and kisses my fingertips. "You never have to buy me anything. Just waking up every morning to your beautiful smile is gift enough for me."

He gently kisses my tears away and leads me to the sofa. Standing in front of the sofa, he kisses my face and neck and slowly unties my robe. He cups my breast gently in his hands and covers my nipple with his mouth. Using his tongue to make circles around my nipple, he pulls it in and out of his mouth.

"Mmm."

We both have on our traditional "I love you" robes with hearts all over them. We wear them every year on Valentine's Day.

I don't know whose robe hits the floor first, but we never sit down on the sofa. We make love on the living room floor.

"I love you. I love you. I love you," is all we keep repeating to each other the entire time we make love.

"I love you. I love you."

The CD is back on our theme song and Prince is professing, "Nothing's forbidden and nothing's taboo. Wheeeeeeeeeen 2 R in love."

We climax together. Explosive.

Distance...
Heart... What?

Keep your eyes wide open before marriage and half-shut afterwards.

—Benjamin Franklin

Asia _____

"Baby, you know if I had any other choice, I'd be here with you. But when business calls, hey." Shaun shrugs his shoulders as he grabs several pairs of Polo briefs out of the drawer and stuffs them in his suitcase. He throws his garment bag on the bed and then walks back to the closet.

"How long will you be gone this time?" I plop down on the edge of the bed and fold my arms in disgust. He just got back from a three week stint in the Cayman Islands.

"Two weeks, until May 2nd."

"May 2nd? Do you know what May 1st is?" I know he must've forgotten like most men do.

"Yes, I know. Your birthday."

"You intentionally made plans to be out of town on my birthday!?"

"Baby, there's nothing I can do. I have several important meeting arranged while I'm in Europe. I can't change them."

"Then I can go with you." I jump off the bed with a newfound enthusiasm now that I had solved that problem. I walk briskly to the closet to pull out my Louis Vouitton luggage.

"Ah, ah, ah, ah. Stop right there." He sits down on our bed and pats his knee. I walk over and sit on his lap. "Asia, you know that your sexy ass is too much of a distraction for me when I got business to take care of. I'll be in the middle of a meeting talking about diamond clarity, cut, color, carat weight and all that bull-shit, and they'd hear a knock coming from under the table." He knocks on the headboard for effect. "You wanna know what that is?

I don't really want to know but I say, "What?" anyway.

"That would be my hard ass dick banging up against the table announcing that I got the sexiest wife in the world and she's waiting in the hostel for me."

I laugh, partly because he can be so funny at times and partly to keep from crying. I don't want to spend my birthday alone. I put my head on his shoulder and he massages the back of my neck.

"Do you think you can move up a meeting or two so that you can be home for my birthday?"

"I'll try to do that. I'm not making any promises, but I'ma try *really* hard to be in and out of Amsterdam. I mean, who wants to be there for two weeks? I bet it's probably going to be packed with silly college students or something crazy like that."

"How horrible," I say frowning at the thought of a bunch of partying college students on spring break.

"Yeah, I know. But anyway, I'm a try to get back early. If not, I promise I'll make it up to you."

"Promise?"

"Scout's honor." He crosses his chest and puts up two fingers. I hit him on the arm, "You weren't a boy scout."

Shaun laughs, "But that doesn't mean that I'm not sincere." He lifts me off his lap to go finish packing.

When we first met, I never thought we'd end up so distant. My sister, India, and I went to Dartmouth College in Hew Hampshire to visit the campus over our high school spring break that was not at the same time as the college's.

India was in her senior year of high school and I was only a sophomore, fifteen. It took a lot of convincing, but we were able to assure my parents that I would keep a curfew and do whatever India told me to do for this week at Dartmouth. Well, she was looking at the campus, but I had bigger and better things in mind.

When I met him that first night at one of the fraternity parties, I thought I had died and gone to heaven. When I gave him my virginity the next night, it was confirmed. Little did we know that we'd be connected for life.

After we left Dartmouth that week, I thought that I would never hear from Shaun again. I was right. He was so deep into his studies that he never had a chance to call and when I called him all I got was the answering machine.

Since planning and organizing is my thing, I mapped out the route I would take to get back to Dartmouth and Shaun. Although I hated school, I worked like a slave my senior year of high school to impress my parents. They had been more than disappointed with my average academic performance and hadn't forgotten about some of the things that I had done the first time I'd gone there that my big-mouthed sister told them. After convincing them that I wouldn't blow their money, Dad pulled some strings to get me in.

When I got there, I forgot all about Shaun. I had one purpose in mind—to get my MRS. While all the other girls were dressed in sweats or jeans with their hair pulled back into a lifeless ponytail because they wanted a B.A., B.S., or something crazy like a J.D., I only wore the finest apparel and frequented the salon weekly. Purse and shoes were coordinated daily. And, since less means more when it comes to jewelry and perfume, I wore very little of both.

I even picked classes according to which ones would have the highest concentration of men. People often underestimate the power of odds. But if I'm in a class where the ratio of men to women is 9:1, the chances of me nabbing my husband un-contested are pretty high.

Now, arranging my "Must Have" list was easy. It included a number of nonnegotiables. Because I was 5'7" without heels, my husband needed to be at least 6'2". A lean, muscular frame would suit my grip quite nicely. The icing on my cake was vanilla. Vanilla mocha topped with a cold black head of curly hair.

He couldn't be a charity case on a full scholarship to the university either. His parents had to be footing the bill for his schooling like my parents were. *Mmm, mmm. A 6-figured lollipop.*

My hunt took me to every event from the high society func-tions to the small sorority gatherings. I moved from being a *Sports for Idiots* candidate to nearly qualifying to referee any football or basketball game. Didn't miss one home game.

This pursuit had me in the library, more than I care to admit, and attending classes so regularly that some of that stuff was trying to stick. Clogging up my brain waves and almost shifting my focus to school. But I got back on track. My husband was there and I was determined to find him.

And then it happened. As I was about to enter the Mandora Glass House for the Christmas celebration, I heard a voice say, "Let me get that." And a big, strong well-manicured hand with long fingers reached around me and pulled the door opened. I turned to thank him, and when I looked up into those onyx eyes all that would come out was, "Mm." *How many licks does it take?*

"Princess. Oh my God, I didn't even recognize you." Shaun's extended hand swallowed mine in a gentle grasp. "How have you been? Where have you been? How long have you been here?" he asked after we had been holding hands for what seemed like too long and not long enough at the same time.

"Let's grab a table so that we can catch up," I suggested.

Time was meaningless. We talked and laughed until the owner came out to ask us if there was anything else he could do for us.

Now that I had located him, it was time to move to the second phase of the plan. Mousetrap. Shaun has always been a lady's man so he was on display at every event. Because he was practically flawless, he was accustomed to getting everything he wanted, when he wanted it. I was determined not to give in so easily to him this time. I was a grown woman, not a high schooler. He would have to wait for my lollipop the second time around. I was on a mission.

I was never too available when he wanted to go on dates. And, I didn't ward off the advances of men when Shaun and I were at the same parties. We were not an official item yet and, until then, he needed to see that other men wanted me too.

Well, nobody wants me now. That's what happens when love blinds you and takes over your master plan. You lose all insight. Everybody knows I belong to Shaun. We've been together forever.

Shaun zips his suitcase and pushes the intercom button, "Ida can you be a sweetheart and send the driver for my luggage?"

"Sure, Mr. Duvall. Anything for you," Ida's smile comes across the wires. "Is there anything else I can do for you?"

"Just one more thing, Ida. I need you to take the rest of the day off. Asia will be ordering out tonight."

I give him a dirty look, but he doesn't look my way. He's just too friendly with the help. I had not considered ordering out.

"Thank you, Mr. Duvall. I'll send the driver up right away."

"No thank you, Ida," Shaun says before hanging up the phone. He turns around, looks at the expression on my face and asks, "What?" Like he doesn't know.

He comes and sits next to me on the bed and puts his arms around me. I laid my head on his shoulders. We sit like that until the driver knocks on the door.

I walk Shaun out to the car and kiss him gently on his lips. He says he'll call me when he gets to Amsterdam. I watch the car zoom down the block and turn the corner.

Back in the condo, I sprawl across our bed and cry. Don't know exactly what I'm crying about, but I cry anyway. When I wake up in the middle of the night, I cry myself back to sleep.

Screwed Up

There are two wolves warring in a man's heart—one is love, one is hate. Which one wins? The one you feed the most.

—African Proverb

Asia____

For the next two days, I don't leave my room. Ida brings me the meal that I request, which is crackers and cheese spread with a bottle of scotch. On the third day, I am going to try something different. I decide to do crackers and peanut butter with my scotch. But before I can call Ida to let her know, I hear her outside my bedroom door.

"Well, just let me tell her first," I hear Ida say before she knocks on my bedroom door. When I don't answer, Ida knocks again, "Mrs. Duvall, it's me, Ida." When she still gets no answer she twists the doorknob and comes in, shutting the door behind her. "Senora Duvall we have a little situation. See, I was expecting a delivery when—"

"Okay, your time is up," Amber says swinging my bedroom door open. "How long does it take to tell her that I'm here?"

"Amber what are you doing up here?" I ask with the energy that only adrenaline could have provided.

"I've been calling you all week and she keeps telling me that you are unavailable."

"I am unavailable. Don't I *look* unavailable to you?"

"You *look* sick," Amber pinches her nose, "and you *smell* sick too. I know what you haven't been doing over the last couple of days."

Amber flounces over to the window and pulls back the curtains, shocking my system with brightness I hadn't seen in a while. Then she opens up the window and lets in the spring breeze.

"I know, don't tell me, my presence is really all the sunshine you need," Amber smiles my way. I frown.

When she notices that Ida is still standing there, she flicks her hand towards the door, "Poof, be gone." Ida quickly leaves the room mumbling under her breath in Spanish.

"Amber no one asked you to come here disrupting things."

"Uh duh, I believe things are already pretty screwed up." She puts both hands on her hips and throws her shoulders back. "Seriously, have you smelled yourself lately?"

I pull the covers over my head, "What do you want? Leave me alone."

"I need a favor," Amber snatches the comforter off the bed and throws it on the floor. I pull the sheet over my head as I hear bath water running.

"What? You need to take a bath?" I point from underneath my

sheet. "There's a full bathroom in the guest room down the hall on the left. Ida can show you where it is."

"No. You need the bath," she yanks the sheet off my head and throws it on the floor next to the comforter. "I need a place to stay for two weeks."

"What?!" I yell and sit straight up in the bed. "Are you out of your mind?"

"Just hear me out," Amber puts her hands up as if she's a crossing guard stopping traffic.

"I don't want or need to hear you. The answer is no."

"But I have no where to go," Amber whines. "I just need two weeks."

"Stay at a hotel. There's one on every corner downtown."

"With work and finals coming up, I can't live out of a room and a suitcase. I need space."

"And I should care because of what?" I ask, doubtful that she would be able to give me an acceptable answer. "Wait, hold that thought. I think I will take that bath now. I need to be coherent for this one." I let the jets of my triangular whirlpool soothe my soul.

Maybe a little company won't be so bad after all.

Expecting the
Unexpected

God could not be everywhere,
so he created Mothers.

—Jewish Proverb

Jazz____

"Ms. Cherrington, have you seen the McAdoo file? I just had it." I release the intercom button and shuffle some of the folders around in a failed attempt to locate the missing file.

Amber strolls over to my desk and pulls out a folder from under the pile of mess that I have made in the two hours that I had been there. "All open cases are in green file folders. Settled cases are in red clamped folders. Pending, yellow." She hands the McAdoo file to me.

"Scary. I think you've been hanging around Asia *waaay* too long. You're starting to think like her."

"As long as I don't start looking like her." Amber smiles, "I'm so much hotter." We laugh.

Amber straightens up my desk. "What's wrong with you anyway? You've been acting pretty strange lately."

"I don't know. I've been trying to figure that out myself." I huff and push back in my chair. "I've been waking up late for work and having to pull myself out of bed. Forgetting every little thing. I would forget my name if it were not on that placard," I say pointing to the nameplate that Chase had bought me when we moved into the new office. "And—"

"And everything makes you nauseous, you haven't drunk your vanilla latte in about two months, your favorite apple strudel tastes funny to you, and you'd prefer to skip lunch than feel like all that food will come up at any minute. Not to mention the fifteen pounds that you've picked up in the last couple of months."

"Fifteen pounds?"

"Okay, fourteen." Amber walks around the desk and pats me on my stomach, "It's called being pregnant."

"Pregnant?!" I yell caught completely off guard by the accusation. "I'm not pregnant. I just went off my menstrual on.....what was the date?"

I flip back through my desk calendar looking for the red dot that I put to track my cycle. I notice all of the cases and meetings I've had over the past few months. I sit back in my chair and try to think about how long all of this has been going on as I search the calendar.

"What month is this? May?"

"June," Amber corrects me. "June 7th."

"Oh, shit! I haven't had a period since March 22nd." I grab the phone and call Chase.

"Hey, baby," he says in a hurried voice, "can I call you right back?"

"I haven't had a period since March."

"March? Damn, I'm on my way."

Chase must have taken a helicopter because he walks into my office in twelve minutes flat with a Walgreen's bag. He pulls out the EPT and smiles. "I wanted to know right away, because I called Dr. Harold Gray and he can't see us until 2:30."

When I try to stand, I realize that my knees are weak. He walks around the desk and grabs my elbow to help me up.

My private bathroom that is located inside my office a few feet from my desk, but it seems to take an eternity to get there. I can't remember ever being this nervous in my life. Not when I took the Bar. Not when I got married. Not ever.

"Jazz, did you hear me?"

"Huh, what? Did you say something baby?"

He walks over and hugs me tightly. Then he kisses me on my forehead. "You ready?"

I nod and watch him take the first pregnancy test out of the twin pack. I sit on the toilet and hold the test where my urine stream will be. My hands are shaking so badly that I almost drop it into the toilet.

Chase takes it out of my hand. "You relax and I'll hold it."

I'm determined not to cry. No matter what the test results are. After I finish, I just sit there with him squatting beside me as we watch the urine saturate the swatch and display the green plus sign in a matter of minutes.

Don't cry, don't cry, don't cry.

Chase leans over and kisses the tears on both cheeks. "Don't cry."

"We're having a—" I choke on the words as the tears continue to roll.

Chase gets a Kleenex and tries wiping my tears away, but doesn't really seem to be into the tear wiping duty as he goes off to some distant land. "Which shade of blue do you like? There's cerulean, azure, sapphire."

I think you may be a little ahead of yourself, I think to myself, but I dare not tell him.

"Indigo may be too dark. Maybe teal."

Although it seems like a 50/50 chance, there are more women in the world than men which make the odds of us having a boy a little less than 50%.

He continues to muse, "And another thing, I'm not buying any of those borders from the store. I'ma paint one wall with a basketball court, one with a football field, and maybe the other one with a golf course. Yeah, golf's good. Tiger's put us on the map."

"Baby, baby, baby...."

"Yeah?"

I stare at him to see if he was back on earth again. I narrow my eyes on him.

"What? Did I say something wrong?" he asks again looking honestly confused.

It's a lost cause trying to tell him that I could possibly have a girl. Whatever. Being surrounded by a basketball court, a football field, and a golf course won't kill her. I walk to the basin to wash my hands. He comes behind me and washes them for me.

"What do you want to do until our doctor's appointment with Dr. Gray? I have a conference call in about fifteen minutes." I want to cancel it and go celebrate.

"I have some research that I need to do on the net. I'll just hang out here until it's time."

We walk out of the office and Amber is waiting there with a big grin on her face. "Well?"

"So when were you going to tell me? You knew before I did," I say feeling like I'm about to cry again.

"Congratulations," Amber says practically singing through every syllable. "Now look," Amber says showing me the catalogue that she had been looking through. "Isn't this the cutest dress you've ever seen?" Amber asks pointing at a white chiffon ruffle dress.

"Ooooh, this is absolutely gorgeous. She can wear this to her christening."

"She?" Chase gives me the eye.

"Just joking, Baby. I really don't care if it's a boy or a girl."

"Huh?" Amber and Chase say in unison.

"As long as it's healthy, I don't care.'

They both look at me with skepticism in their eyes.

"I don't." Their expressions don't change. I dismiss their disbelief with a wave of my hand.

"Anyway Amber, we have a conference call. We need to head over to the...uh...whatever the name of that room is." I kiss Chase and turn towards the door.

"Yeah, I need to call Shaun anyway and let him know that I can't meet him in Amsterdam," Chase says as we head for the door.

"Amsterdam? Y'all was just there. He might as well apply for citizenship as much as he's there," I shake my head.

"Yeah, well he went back and he found a buyer for 'Beauty in Amsterdam'. A museum wants to pay $75,000 for it."

I stop so abruptly that he runs right into me as he is searching his cell phone for Shaun's number. "Honey, that is wonderful. When were you going to tell me?"

"How'd you think I got here so fast? I was parking the car when you called. He had just told me an hour before. But, I guess it wasn't meant to be."

"Okay, we both can't be losing our minds at the same time. Now what in your mind tells you that you can turn down that type of money?"

"No, I'm not going to turn it down. I'll just have to ship it."

"Ship a $75,000 painting?"

"It's safe."

"It's safer if you take it. I mean, it's not like you're going to be gone forever.

"Yeah, but you need me right now."

"And I'ma need you for the next eighteen-years and five months or so. So don't think you're missing out by being gone a couple of days." I elbow him in the ribs and then as an afterthought I ask, "You are only going to be gone a couple of days, right?"

"I become suicidal if I'm away from you any longer than that." He bends down and gives me a long kiss and adds a tongue.

"Ugh, corny," Amber says. "Can we leave before you two make another baby up in here? Well, y'all didn't make the baby in here did you?"

We both open our mouths to say something, but Amber raises her hand, "Don't answer that. I don't wanna know."

Chase and I look at each other and laugh as we walk out of my office.

In the conference room, I decide to call Asia before my partners come in. After five rings, she picks up the phone sounding like she was just run over by a Mac truck.

"Asia? What's wrong with you? You sound horrible. Are you sick?"

"No, no, just sleeping." Asia says.

"In the middle of the day? That's pretty sick, even if you're not," I laugh but Asia seems to be in a slump.

"What's up girl?" she asks.

"I'm pregnant!"

She lets out a little giggle. "Girl, it sounded like you said you're pregnant. What did you say?"

"Exactly," I yell into the phone.

"Oh my God, Jazz! How wonderful!"

There's the enthusiasm that I'm usta hearing from my girl. She starts throwing the questions left and right.

"How many months are you?"

"I am..."

"When did you find out?"

"Well it....."

"Why am I just hearing about this?" she snaps. "How long have you known? God I need to start planning the baby shower."

She will find a reason to plan a party.

As she rattles off a few more questions, I call her name, "Asia....Asia....Asia...."

"What?"

"Do you want to continue rambling to yourself or would you like for me to answer any of the questions that you just asked?"

Pink Ruffles

People are like stained-glass windows. They sparkle and shine when the sun is out, but when the darkness sets in, their true beauty is revealed only if there is a light from within.

—Elizabeth Kubler Ross

Amber_____

"Pink ruffled panties lying on the floor? Why is there blood on my panties? I rubbed my eyes. Didn't quite know what to make of that and I had no one to ask. I sat up in my bed to go pick them up and pain shot up through my girlie part. I laid back down with my hands cupping my girlie part to try and stop the throbbing. It was all coming back to me.

"My mother always said, 'Don't let nobody touch ya' pussy, Girl. Nobody but me or ya' daddy can touch you.' She had only been dead for a week now and I didn't know what to do. Is this what she meant? Daddy can touch me like this? Is this how it's supposed to be? She said that only her and daddy could touch it so it must be okay, right?

"The door to my room swung opened and my daddy stepped in and kicked my baby doll out of his way.

'Whatcha sitting there crying fa'? Huh?'

I grabbed my *Wonder Woman* blanket and pulled it up to my chin for protection.

'What the hell you think that's gon do, you lil' heifer? Here I am trying ta' make you feel better and forget about cho' momma and you ack like I den done something bad t' ya.' He tried to step forward, but wobbled a little before he grabbed the doorknob."

"How old were you?" Dr. Pleasant asks, catching me off guard because I really hadn't been talking to her. Not really.

"Ten."

"Ten," she scribbles on her notepad. "So did you tell anyone?"

"I'm telling you now," I snap. *Can't believe I let this slip out.*

"No back then. Who did you tell? This was what?" She flips through my chart. "Twelve years ago. You had to have somebody to talk to."

My gaze shoots daggers at her, while I try to delete her ugly ass and my pink ruffle panties with the bloodstain from my mental rolodex. *What a quack.*

One thing that was visible on the last piece of paper that I took out of the safe was Louisiana Rock Adoption Agency. The adopted child was a baby girl adopted by Leroy and Ester Sykes with my birthday on the certificate.

"So you were ten. How long did the abuse last?"

The timer on my watch sounds at almost the exact time that the last grain of sand falls in her hourglass. I stand and head for the door.

"Amber, there are only two sessions left before your assignment is complete and you are released from this program." She takes off her wire rim glasses and places them on her desk. "I have to approve your release. And in order to do that, I need to believe that you are not a heartless, vicious killer anymore."

I slowly turn back around to face her to see where she is going with this conversation.

"This organization only takes in malicious killers. You knew that from the beginning. You've been under the wrong treatment plan if you're a victim of molestation. Why did you wait so long to tell me this?"

"When I first got here, I had nobody. I needed a place to live, someone to take care of me, someone to usher me into adulthood. All of that was covered here."

"But you haven't been counseled for the issues that you have."

"I don't need the organization anymore. I can take care of myself."

"I'm sorry Amber. I have to sign off on your release and I'm going to have to extend your stay because—"

She's shocked to find herself dangling in the air with my hands around her throat.

"6348 North Clariton Avenue," I say through clenched teeth. "Nadia, seven. Tré, four," I fix my eyes on hers so that she can grasp the gravity of the situation, and her eyes divert to a Christmas photo of her children.

Her eyes bulge with fear. I drop her to her feet. She grabs her throat gasping for air.

"Lexington Retirement Village. William and Cybil Pleasant. Raleigh, North Carolina."

She looks up at me. "Amber, we can fix this. I promise, we'll do some rush sessions. It won't be much longer. You don't have to do this. You need help."

"A twin right?" I pick up the photo off her desk of the two of them smashing cake in each other's faces on their 21st birthday. "Her name's Jacquelyn?"

"Amber, you're not ready."

I slam her photo face down on the desk and hear the glass shatter. "I kill by choice. I'm not a malicious killer randomly killing innocent victims. I haven't killed one person who didn't deserve to die."

She shakes her head and looks even more scared than when I had her by the throat. "And that's what you're missing, Amber. We don't kill to take lives. We kill to save them."

Okay, she fucked me up with that fortune cookie proverb.

"This session is over. I hope that we don't have to revisit this topic again. Do you get the picture?" I storm out of her office.

Fortune Cookie Proverb

I submit that an individual who breaks a law that conscience tells him is unjust, and who willingly accepts the penalty of imprisonment in order to arouse the conscience of the community over its injustice, is in reality expressing the highest respect for the law.

—Dr. Rev. Martin Luther King, Jr.

Amber____

Karob is finishing his session up at the same time. We look at each other and I walk behind him to the elevator. *Boy you make them Diesel Keever jeans look like paradise uncut.* He puts his key in the override access slot and pushes the 40th floor.

I divert my eyes to the elevator buttons when he turns around to look at me.

"How did it go?" he asks, as he always does.

"The same." I answer as I always do. Only this time I'm lying. This time I feel something. And he knows it. Something is still churning in the pit of my stomach that has to come out. I haven't talked about or thought about any of my past since I left from that house the day of my adopted father's funeral. It's sorta become a figment of my imagination. And it gets blurrier and blurrier. Maybe I made it all up is what I had began thinking. It seems so distant.

I rotate my neck to release some of the images that are trying to come back. As I follow Karob to the conference room, I wipe the one lone tear that threatens to fall from my eye. *Your crying days are over. Suck it up.*

We sit in our respective chairs and wait for the meeting to start. The theatre screen is lowered from its encasement in the ceiling and pops on. We're greeted by a deep, calming voice that seems to be more appropriate for lulling a baby to sleep than for briefing assassins. Me and Karob secretly call him "The Voice."

"Well, we're finally at the end. And nobody's gotten hurt."

Karob and I look at each other both knowing that ignorance is bliss and knowledge is painful. We are hurting more than he'll ever know.

The screen shows a well dressed African and his entourage walking on Broadway and Seventh through Times Square. "This is Olukumah Achere Ugwu. Nigerian." The Voice says. "This is the man on the ground that profited from Operation Discreet Massacre. He obtained passports, arranged travel for the men, hotel accommodations, and took care of their families in their brief absences."

The screen now shows a slide show of different still shots of Ugwu. "Over a ten year period, Ugwu brought over 3,000 Nigerians to Panama under the guise of them being case studies for DNA lineage research. In actuality, they were lab rats for HIV and AIDS testing."

"Well, there had to be a surge in passport request. That didn't send off a red flag to the lead officials in the country?" Karob relaxes his face to remove the skepticism from his brow.

"Remember, many of these Nigerians had never seen that type of money. And Ugwu made it very inviting. Paying them in advanced for their services and offering to "hire" others in their family if they worked out. Everyone was paid well, from the top down."

"Didn't the families notice that the men who went with him were the ones getting sick?" Karob leans back in his chair and folds his arms while studying the images.

"Not initially," The Voice says, "because the men were given a three-year supply of medication to treat and suppress any symptoms while their wives and girlfriends who they brought the HIV virus home to had none. It appeared at the time that the women were infecting the men."

An aerial shot of a mass grave is shown. "Women were killed on the spot for any signs or symptoms of this unknown illness. Just the common cold could cause you to lose your life."

"Which probably kept a lot of people from going to the doctor which in turn spread the disease even more," Karob's eyes stay glued to the screen.

"Exactly," says The Voice.

The screen now shows images of sick woman and babies in makeshift hospitals. Women and children filled all the beds, were sitting on the ground in and around the tent, as well as lined up for the white American doctors to treat the untreatable. Many women are pushing infants and toddlers to the doctors or nurses to examine, but with there being so many, they had to wait their turn. It probably was too late.

The Voice continues, "The connection wasn't made until years later when Ugwu tried to take another group of men to Panama and people refused because it was then common knowledge that all the men who had gone with him before were dead along with many of their family members. Wiped out whole villages."

"And infected thousands, I'm sure," Karob shakes his head. I see a glint of anger in his eyes.

"Last count, over 117,000 Nigerians had died in connection with Mission Discreet Massacre. Most of them were children and infants. It's harder for their immune system to fight against all the different infections. And without proper medication, it was a miserably, painful death."

"So why is he in New York?" Karob asks.

"Member of the Nigerian Delegation to the UN Commission on Human Rights. They're meeting in New York City this week."

Irony at its best, I think.

"And what's with all the body guards?" Karob asks staring intently at each shot of Ugwu. Karob never asks this many questions. He's usually as detached as I am. Get the background info, get the mission, and do the job. This is really out of character.

"There have been several attempts on his life. All failed,

obviously. This is his first visit to the U.S. and we want to send him out with a bang. Literally."

Karob and I look at each other. *We like things that go boom.*

"We have to send a message loud and clear," The Voice continues. "We've already sent two of the companies who benefited from this massacre into bankruptcy with financial scandals. We were able to be subtle with Dr. Lewis because he was nothing but hired help. A medical doctor who had a debt to somebody. We don't even believe that he knew what he was injecting at first. Senator Warren was only the political liaison that kept the project under the radar, allowing American companies to experiment with human lives. Neither Lewis nor Warren profited financially; however, everyone involved will be able to put two and two together and come up with four and know that there's someone out here who will not stand for the massacre of innocent people for scientific research."

A real time shot shows Ugwu having dinner at Sylvia's in Harlem talking and laughing like he doesn't have a care in the world. The Voice continues, "No one really knows of Ugwu's involvement. Because Ugwu wasn't sitting in on the planning meetings, wasn't calling shots. He was only a pawn. The first line of defense that must be broken. But he was the most important piece to the puzzle because none of this could have been possible without an "Ugwu" on the ground!" The Voice yells.

I don't think I've ever heard him yell.

"No one knows except the people who suspect it in Africa. The ones dead and the ones alive."

"And we can avenge them both," I stare at the screen as it zooms in on Ugwu. "So blow 'em up or shoot 'em? Which one?"

The sooner we get this over with, the sooner, I can put this part of my life in a box on the shelf with the rest of my forgotten pink panty memories.

For the next ten hours, we are studying the history of Nigeria, bios of everyone who we may encounter, floor plans, and a billion other tidbits of information which is all taught to us in Swahili, one of the several languages that Ugwu speaks.

Then we are put under. For each mission, we are hypnotized and given the details while unconscious. That way, we won't forget anything. It's a lot of information. After another hour, Karob and I leave, knowing that we'd have another twelve hour day tomorrow.

Going down in the elevator, Karob says to me, "I killed my father."

When we finally make it to the ground level, I loop my arm in his as we exit the elevator, "So did I."

Our heels click to the same beat as we leave the building.

A Whale
or a Walrus

A true friend never gets in your way
unless you happen to be going down.
—Arnold H. Glasgow

Asia____

I can't remember the last time Shaun had been home for longer than a week at a time. He'd come in after being out of the country for half the month or an entire month and then be gone again within a week. I beg him to stop working so much. I offer to go with him. I even told him that I would work as his assistant while we're on the road. He shot down every suggestion that I've made. Now I'm sitting in the house with nothing to do. Again.

I pick up the phone and call Jazz, and when she picks up the phone, I say, "How soon can you meet me at Nick's?"

Jazz moans as if she can taste the food, "Ooow, that sounds good. I'm starving. I can be there in an hour."

"Make it two. A girl has to primp and prepare," I say already looking in the mirror and lifting my lifeless hair.

"Make it one or you'll be eating alone."

———

Without looking at my caller id, I answer and sigh, *"Yeessss, Jazz?"*

"Don't act like you're irritated by *my* call. You're the one who's twenty minutes late, Asia."

"I'm only seventeen minutes late. And anything under a half hour is still considered fashionable. And if you weren't so early—"

"Early and on time are two different things. Now, where are you?"

"Right behind you."

Jazz whirls around, snaps her flip closed, and rolls her eyes back like she does when she's disgusted and happy at the same time. "You know you're trifling, right?"

I hug her and kiss her on both cheeks, before bowing down to the king. I hope it's a boy. I put both my hands on her stomach, "Hey Lil' Man. Auntie Asia is here now so we can get started. But you better get used to waiting for your Auntie because cute people take a little longer to prepare than your average Joe Blow." I cut my eyes at Jazz and she slaps my hands off her stomach. I laugh and sit across from her in our usual booth.

"Did you forget how crowded Nick's is for lunch? I had to name drop just to get to stand in the entryway."

She has a point. Nick's Seafood Restaurant is one of the finest in Chicago. Décor and ambiance aside, the waiters in tuxedoes add flair that is unmatched anywhere within a fifty mile radius. And, with it being centrally located downtown on Clark Street, it's hard to get a reservation.

"Okay, I promise, promise, promise that next time—"

"Next time what?" Skepticism is always Jazz's strong suit. It's the attorney in her.

"Next time I'll only be ten minutes late. Deal?" I show my best glamour girl smile and offer my hand to call a truce. Jazz slaps away my hand and laughs. I'm forgiven.

"Did you place my order?" I ask.

"Chilean Sea Bass in soy sake sauce."

"That's my girl. You know exactly what I want," I lick my lips at the thought of eating the succulent fish.

"That's because you never order anything different."

The waiter comes over for our drink orders. "Good afternoon, Mrs. Duvall, Mrs. Livingston."

"Hello, Delleon," we sing in unison.

"Will you have your usual drinks?"

"I think I'ma take a walk on the wild side. Momma over there will have Evian." I joke.

When I pick up the extensive drink menu, Jazz raises her eyebrow at me. I pretend not to notice as I concentrate on finding something to soothe my soul. I finally order the San Antonio Cardinale from California.

"Would you like the bottle?" Delleon asks.

"Yes, that would be wonderful. And a decanter, if you don't mind. I need my wine to breathe a little before I drink it." I ball up my fists and open them in illustration.

"Of course, Mrs. Duvall," he says before he rushes off.

"So you need the whole bottle, huh? What's going on with you?"

"Nothing. Just thirsty."

"They have Evian," Jazz jokes but doesn't laugh. "Look Asia, I don't know what's going on with you, but you've been doing a heck of lot of drinking in the last six months. Come on, spit it out."

"There's nothing to tell. Everything is fine," I say and smile in hopes of moving on.

"Well, I just have one thing to say. I've never met a cute alcoholic." We laugh and Jazz continues, "They may start out cute but they don't stay cute for long. And I just wanna warn you ahead of time since you're not the average Joe Blow."

Just then, Delleon comes back with the bottle of red wine and sits it, along with the flute, on the table. Then, using the cork screw, he pops the cork. He pours the wine into the decanter before racing off.

A couple of minutes later, Delleon comes back and pours the Cardinale into my flute. I pick up my glass to admire the depth of the wine's color. As I swirl the wine in the glass, I say, "Now you never told me about finding out you were pregnant. And don't leave out anything. Was it planned or a surprise?"

"Both if that makes sense," Jazz's smile spreads widely across her face and her dimples find their home in her cheeks. "Me and

Chase had been trying to get pregnant for a few months." She is practically bouncing in her seat. Her glow seems to permeate on the outside of her body and scream to the world that she is thoroughly satisfied with life.

"We bought the ovulation kit a few months ago. We'd been counting days, taking temperatures," she leans forward and whispers, "and fucking like rabbits." Her Cheshire grin becomes wider. "Does that sound good or what?"

"Which part?" I ask frowning. Looking like a whale before a baby or a walrus after?"

"You know you're not human," she laughs and wags a disappointed finger at me. "And if you are, you're definitely not a woman. It's what we were put here to do."

Shit, is she about to get on her soapbox? I pour myself some more wine.

"To multiply, create. To plant a seed. I know you don't think I was put here to be a lawyer and for you to be a........." she motions her hands as if searching for the right word. "What do you do again?" We laugh before she continues.

"No, but seriously Asia, can you *honestly* tell me that you never want to have kids? To breathe life into another human being?"

I take a look around the restaurant and focus on the abstract wall painting that any two-year old could have done, "Shaun and I decided that it's not the right time for us. Maybe it'll never be."

Jazz raises a perfectly arched brow, "Did I ask about what *Shaun* wants or what *you* want?"

"You know, Shaun and Chase are two different breeds. Just because they're best friends don't mean that they share the same values," I say.

"Yes or no, because I can think of twenty ways for you to have a baby without Shaun's consent."

I wave my hand at her. "All that ass wiping, vomiting, and crying. Giving up my beauty sleep to do what? Uh, uh, nobody could love motherhood as much as they claim to. Besides, Shaun makes a good point. He wants us to have enough money to make sure our kids are set for life."

Delleon places the bread on the table. The sourdough bread saves me. Hopefully we'll move on to another topic. I quickly unwrap the bread and spread on the butter.

"Mm, mm, mm. I forgot how good their bread is."

Jazz grabs a piece and dips it in the warm olive oil and gets right back to the topic at hand. "How much more money does he think he needs?" she bites the bread and moans.

"I don't know, but he's out of the country more than he's in and when he's here, half of his time is wrapped up in late night meetings. If we wanted to make a baby, it would be hard right now with his busy schedule. I'm lucky if I get it once a month."

"God, you poor baby," Jazz rests her hand on my shoulder consoling me. "I think I would kill myself if I didn't get it at least four times a week. No wonder you've turned to the bottle." She laughs. "As a matter of fact, I'ma make sure Delleon gives you one of these bottles to go." She taps my bottle of Cardinale and still laughing says, "Put it on the pillow next to you. It's a gift from me. Consider it a postcard from paradise."

"Oh, that's funny, huh? Let's see who's laughing in about six months at three and four in the morning."

Just then, Delleon comes with our food. He spreads the cloth napkins across our laps before he places our food on the table. "Is there anything else I can get for you ladies?"

"No everything looks great, Delleon. Thanks," Jazz says.

Citrus Ginger Salmon is the second best entrée at Nick's after the Chilean Sea Bass. I take my fork and reach across the table to break off a small piece of Jazz's salmon. Their secret orange ginger cream sauce used to sautéed the fish is full of flavor. It practically melts on my tongue.

We stay at the restaurant for another hour just catching up. We order another bottle of wine for me and dessert for her.

Jazz says she has to use the restroom. She hops up and struts proudly across the room overly emphasizing the little pooch that she has. *I know that has to be her 17th time going,* I laugh.

I am still snickering when Delleon comes with our check. I give him my credit card to pay the bill. While I'm waiting for him to come back, my phone chimes.

A video text? I didn't even know I had that feature. I push the view button.

"Oh my God!" I cover my mouth and I look at the images before me, then I jump up and run towards the exit.

"Mrs. Duvall, Mrs. Duvall, you forgot your credit card," I hear Delleon call, but I can't go back. I just can't.

Lotta Things Worse
Than Death

*Did it ever strike you on such a morning as this
that drowning would be happiness and peace?*

—Charles Dickens

Asia____

I don't think I've ever been in a liquor store. But after I ran out
on Jazz, I stop on my way home. *Whew! Do they all smell
like....like....what's that smell? Is that urine I smell?* Whatever.
Cheap tequila is all I need right now. The 1800 Gold should do
just fine.

"No, no, no, no Miss, you tan't do dat tere Miss," the Korean
guy at the register yells as I yank off the plastic seal and remove the
cork. I turn the bottle up and take my first swig as I walk out of the
store to my car. *God, that burns.*

"That's my kinda woman," some man slurs as the liquor drips down my chin.

I wipe my mouth on the sleeve of my pastel Roberto Cavalli blouse that I got when Shaun took me for a shopping spree on the Via dei Calzaiuoli in Florence.

"Don't drink and drive. It'll kill you." One of the drunkards says to the amusement of all the others. "I should know cuz I died last night." They laugh even louder this time.

I walk over to the seven men sitting on the ledge outside of the liquor store each with his own paper bag and tell them, "There's a lotta things worse than death." This quiets the comedy show and I can tell that it kinda messes up their buzz. Many of them nod like that revelation is one they can relate to. I take another swig of my tequila and hop in my silver convertible S500 Mercedes-Benz.

By the time I make it home, I am feeling no pain. I walk into the condo, flip on the light in foyer, and trip. "Oops." I look to see what I tripped over, but there's nothing there. Just a natural trip over air.

"Hahahahaha," I laugh and quickly cover my mouth as if I expect to wake up somebody, deciding to snicker instead. *Okay, Missy, that's your cue to slow down.* I laugh and turn the tequila bottle up again. It doesn't burn going down my throat anymore. *Hallelujah.* I kick off my Salvatore Ferragamoes at the door. The wall helps me balance myself to my room.

"I don't have to deal with this shit anymore. I'm Asia god-damnit. ASIA! There's a better life waiting for me somewhere."

When I finally make it to my bedroom, I breathe a sigh of relief for not breaking anything valuable on the way and I guess that breath is all my body needs to lurch my tequila along with my lunch in reverse. I make it to the toilet just in time. When I finish throwing up, I stand up and look at myself in the mirror.

"I'm pretty," I say to my reflection. *Well, not with this chunk of puke on my lip.* I grab a Kleenex, wipe my mouth, then reexamine myself. "I'm not fat. I'm fun to be around. So why?"

When no answer comes, I become angry. I pick up the marble soap dispenser and throw it at the mirror and watch the glass shatter. The reflection staring back at me this time is a more accurate representation of who I am or at least who I've become.

Boy, I sound philosophical. I smile blankly at the disfigured face. *I should have drunk the cheap tequila a long time ago.*

I open the medicine cabinet and take out the bottle of sleeping pills that I had bought to help me sleep while Shaun is out of town for three quarters of the year. It's about half full. Probably, fifty or more pills. I pour as many as can fit in my hand, throw them back in my mouth, and wash them down with my 1800 Gold. I do this three, four, or eight times. Who knows? Who can count while drinking this stuff? When the pill bottle is empty and I realize I'm still standing, I open Shaun's medicine cabinet and take out his antique, Diamond-edge straight razor just in case the pills don't work as fast as I had hoped.

After about seven seconds, I decide, "Yeah, this is taking *waaaay* too long."

I take the razor and slit my left wrist. Just as I'm about to cut the right one, everything goes dark.

Amber____

New York went without incident. Me and Karob eliminated the problem and closed out the debt we owed to the organization. Now maybe, just maybe, we can lead normal lives. I'll head to law school and he can prepare to become a history professor. He'll make a good history professor. I'd go to class everyday to listen to his fine ass.

Neither of us has ever slept on the plane on our way to or from a mission. However, this time, we both sleep from JFK to O'Hare. I rested my head on his shoulder and he laid his cheek on my head. Everything seems like it's about to be real cool.

That's why I don't like the feeling I have when Karob escorts me to my door. He hugs me tightly, then looks deeply, searchingly into my eyes before passionately kissing me. This is our first unstaged kiss.

Inside, I close the door behind me, put my back against it smiling as I had seen on many movies. Now I understand the smile. But I don't have time to bask in my newfound joy because, my heart instantly, instinctively sinks to my stomach.

What's wrong with you? You have no reason to feel anything but relief. But relief is not what I'm feeling right now.

I slowly slip out of my Ferragamo sling backs. Well, I guess they're technically Asia's. Technically. She has over 500 pairs of shoes. She won't miss these.

I tilt my head to the side, listening with my ears, but mainly with my heart. I drop my bags to the floor and run to Asia's room. I don't bother knocking, but just burst through the door and snatch the covers off her bed. When she isn't there, I am momentarily stomped because my instincts are always right. Always. I plop down on her bed and giggle at my inability to accept normalcy, happiness.

Okay, I'm dead if she finds me in her room.

I can hear her now, even though it's been more difficult for her to be mean to me lately even when she tries. "Amber, is there something you need that Ida can't help you with?" Then I would pull out her favorite classic, Casablanca. She can never resist. I'd hop in her bed and pull the Egyptian cotton up to my chin.

"You, chaise," she'd say, pointing, just to hold some of the ground that she's lost in my extended stay. That's fine with me. I just want to hang with her. I don't even like Casablanca.

I get up off her bed and, as I'm going towards the door, I see a foot on the floor hanging out of the master bathroom. I seem to float to the bathroom where Asia lies unconscious on the floor. Why can't I see anything? Tears? My vision is lost behind a coats of tears.

No! No! No! This couldn't be happening. Not now! I fall down to my knees and shake her, "Asia, Asia." She's not responding. I begin crying and can't think. *Amber, snap out of it,* I yell to myself.

I pick up the cordless phone off the bathroom counter and dial 911 as I simultaneously open the door to the linen closet to grab a white towel to stop the blood that's pouring from her wrist. Thank God she only did one wrist. That's when I notice the empty bottle of pills in the sink and the expensive bottle of tequila on the counter.

Oh No! No! Oh God no! I snatch up the bottle and look at it.

Sleeping pills? I drop back to the floor and put my head to her chest. Her breathing is shallow. "Shit!"

I take the Narcan out of my jacket pocket. After I locate a vein, I hesitate. I don't know nothing. How long she's been out? How much she took? Does this even work for all drug overdoses?

This Narcan was supposed to be for the Nigerian, Ugwu, if he tried to commit suicide by swallowing some high potency opiate. She's not going to make it. I find a vein and inject the Narcan. Asia instantly inhales and opens her eyes.

I look up to the heavens, "Thank you God." But before the words are outta my mouth good, she closing them again.

"Oh no you don't." I slap her face. I always thought I'd get some kind of pleasure out of that. "Asia, wake up! Come on. Just stay with me until the paramedics get here."

I lift her off the floor, put her in the shower, and turn on the cold water. It keeps her lucid. "Stay with me. Just stay awake." Two minutes later, Terrence, the conseiour, brings in the paramedics, a man and a woman.

"How long has she been out?" the woman asks with urgency in her voice as she turns off the shower and puts the stethoscope to her heart.

"I got here about fifteen minutes ago. She was already unconscious." My voice is breaking up.

"Just a slit wrist?" the man asks talking faster than the woman had as they lift Asia onto the dolly.

"She took these," I say as I pass the paramedic the empty bottle of sleeping pills, "and was unconscious before I gave her a shot of Narcan."

"You a medic?" the woman asks.

"Yeah," I lie.

"Well, you may have just saved her life."

They quickly roll her out. I run out behind them and hop in the back of the ambulance. The sirens blare as we whip through the empty Chicago streets.

I hold Asia's hand and kiss it. "You're not going to die on me. I'm not gonna lose you." There's that blinding coat of tears. I can't stop the flow this time. I pull out my cell phone, scroll down, and push send.

"Hello."

With a trembling voice I say, "Momma Spears."

"Amber? What is it?"

"It's Asia," I muffle a whimper.

Asia's mother starts crying before I tell her anything that has happened and without a question or an explanation given says, "We're on our way."

Lipstick, Dinner & Movies

I think we have to own the fears that we have of each other, and then, in some practical way, some daily way, figure out how to see people differently.

—Alice Walker

Amber____

The mood in the hospital is somber as everyone takes shifts. No one wants to leave even when their time is up, but is forced to at least go shower and eat. There has to be someone there when Asia wakes up. Everyone is emotional.

India is a mess. Half the time we have to put her out of the room because she can't stop crying. "But she's my little sister. I shoulda seen this coming. I shoulda been more supportive. I shoulda done a lotta things different. A lotta things different. I feel so guilty." She covers up her face and cries into her hands. "She supported me when me and Ralph had hard times. She was never judgmental and always had something positive to say. Some way to lift my spirits." It was always some variation of that story before she would start crying again. And out she had to go. Layla usually escorts her out.

The restroom is my refuge when I feel like I want to cry. After I finish holding back my tears, I would clean myself up really good before I'd come back out. Each time, Momma Spears would hug me and rock me a little from side to side. I can't hide nothing from her. She's just so grateful that I made it there in time to save her baby. I'm glad my timing was on point too. Me and Asia have become really close in the past couple of months. I don't want to lose this feel good spot that we've found between us.

Asia has been unconscious for three days. Shaun hasn't even tried to come or call to check on her and no one in the family asks about him. He knows by now because I told Jazz and, of course, Jazz told Chase. Jazz and Chase have been up here every day.

When I went back home to search Asia's room to see if I can figure out what had upset her to the point of suicide, I find the answer on her cell phone. Someone had sent her a fifteen second video of Shaun having an affair. The scene suggests a ménage a trois with the three wine glasses. The third person was holding the camera. Shaun was pushing the woman's head into a pillow, inadvertently concealing her identity, as he banged her doggie style from behind before he climaxes. Shaun looks into the camera and smiles.

Fucking asshole.

Momma Spears is there when Asia wakes up. When I get to the hospital room, everyone is standing around her bed, Momma and Papa Spears, India and Ralph, Jason and Layla, Asia's grandparents, Jazz and Chase. Everybody's talking to Asia.

For someone who has been unconscious for three days, she looks good. The color hasn't quite left her cheeks and her eyes are clear and focused. The only obvious problem is her voice, which is probably scratchy from the tube used to pump her stomach. It sounds raspy and Momma Spears keeps giving her water for lubrication; eventually, her voice becomes clearer. I sit in a chair in the back of the room. After all the small talk, Asia starts rambling.

"I just hate this life," Asia looks toward the window that is blocked by her grandparents.

Every time she makes one of these type of comments, somebody tries to convince her that everything will be alright. They'd talk a little while longer and she'd slip back into her suicidal, depression thingy, saying stuff like, "Nobody cares about me. Nobody loves me."

When people run out of things to comfort her, I decide to give it a try. I stand up. "I love you, Mommie." My knees seem too weak to hold the weight of my admission. I immediately wish I could swallow the words and sit back down in my chair, unnoticed.

"You don't love me, Amber," Asia says sounding disappointed by her realization.

Everyone turns to look at me in surprise.

"What did she say?" asks India.

"Did she just call her 'Mommie'?" asks Asia's grandmother.

"I knew it. I knew it." Momma Spears says with joy in her voice and covers her mouth in shock. "If my grandmother had a twin, she wouldn't look more like her than Amber."

"You just love the money that I give you every month," Asia continues with tears streaming down her face.

I open my purse and take out my wallet. "You talking about this money?" I pull out the money orders that she has given me over the years and walk over to her bed.

I peel the first money order off the stack and show it to her, "To Amber Cherrington. $2,000. Signed, Asia Duvall. June 2003." I show her the next one, "July 2003. August 2003. Do I need to go on? This is every last one of them." I slam them down on her bed. "I didn't want your money." I shake my head. "I never cashed any of them! I wanted you!" I point at her.

Realizing that I'm hollering, I lower my voice, "The only way I could see you, the only way I was allowed to see you, at least once a month was to take this money." I pick up a few of the money orders and shake my fist.

"But all the money in the world can't compare to these couple of months that I've spent with you. This has been the best time of my miserable life. Watching movies and eating dinner together. Shopping and having you tell me which outfit I should or shouldn't wear to work. You fixing a strand of my hair that's out of place." I see a slight smile on Asia's lips. "Or me sneaking in your room and taking your favorite lipstick because I like how good it looks on you. Wondering if it's possible that I will ever be as beautiful as you. That's what I love." I toss the money orders on her hospital bed and several of them fall on the floor. "This money means nothing to me."

I can't see. My vision is blurring up again. *Suck it up, Amber. Your crying days are over.* I can't cry in front of these people. I turn to run out of the door, but a pair of strong hands grabs me and pulls me back. I find my head on the chest of Papa Spears and my body shakes as I cry the cry that I had been holding in all my life.

Momma Spears walks up and is hugging me from behind and rocking me, "Everything's going to be alright, Baby. I promise. Everything will be alright." Now she's crying.

"Amber, come here," Asia says. I wipe my eyes on the back of my hand and I walk over to her bed. She looks up at me with a feeling in her eyes that I can't identify.

"When I gave you away all those years ago, I emotionally shut down," she looks down and starts to twirl the end of her favorite blanket that I brought from home so that she would have a little comfort when she woke up. She hates cheap sheets.

"The love I had for you while you were growing inside of me and then when I looked into those gorgeous eyes when you were born was the ultimate. I cried myself to sleep every night for years after I gave you away. I've been searching for the type of love I felt for you ever since I lost you."

She looks up at me and pats the bed for me to sit next to her. "Amber, every time I see you, I get so angry. Not at you. You're wonderful. Funny, beautiful, insightful. I'm mad at myself because I messed up and missed out on so much of your life. It hurts my heart that I can't get that time back. It is really tearing me apart inside."

Now Asia's crying, along with a whole lotta snifflers behind me. She holds her arms out to me and I gladly go to accept my first hug from my mother. Oddly, it feels comfortable, familiar. I like it. I like her.

I feel Momma Spears come up behind me, then Papa Spears. I see Asia's grandparents put their arms around Asia. Eventually this turns into one big group hug. *Yeah, I can get usta this.*

All Nighter

The main goal of the future is to stop
violence. The world is addicted to it.

—Bill Cosby

Chase____

The tinted windows of the '86 Accord has protected my
identity up to this point. I pull my ski mask down over my
face before I step out of the car. Using one of the only two keys
known to man for this place, I open the door and walk to the
upper-level.

The warehouse is cold, damp, and empty. Nothing. Except for
a bunch of scrap metal and a couple of gutted old cars. The bottom
level is one huge open space with makeshift furniture for comfort.
A bunch of crates with quilted blankets over them for cushion.
Newspapers sprawled across more crates function as the card
table plenty of nights in here. Black paint covers the windows

inside as well as out and cardboard is stuffed in front of the windows. No light will ever escape. Not that there's much light in here anyway. There's one lone light bulb hanging by a rope and an extension cord that goes to who knows where.

Dinnertime. Officers Menendez and Washington are both chained to tables on opposite ends of the warehouse for their third and final meal of the day. Cheesecake Factory. They get to order whatever they want for dinner each night. Breakfast and lunch, they have no choice.

Officer Menendez is just finishing his last bite of cheesecake when Reverend Pookie strides in. I guess in his world, he's dressed to the nines, wearing all red from his pin-striped suit to his snake skin shoes and felt top hat. *Looks like a damn beet.* When he gets to the table where Menendez is, he pulls out a hand-kerchief from his breast pocket and wipes off the edge of the table before he sits on it.

"Hey Pig, you ready t' go home t' ya' family today?" Reverend Pookie asks as he pulls his cigar out of his pocket and licks it.

"Fuck you, Nigga!" Officer Menendez yells at Reverend Pookie and jumps up from the table to confront him, but is restrained by the chains at his wrist.

"Well don't ever say I ain't never tried t' do nuttin fa' ya'." He snaps his fingers at Leonard and Ed, the muscle standing off to the side watching the exchange. "String 'em up."

"No, no. Please no more," Officer Menendez screams. "I can't take it no more."

Reverend Pookie who is heading for the exit, stops and spins around in an about face move to tell Menendez, "Even if you was t' sing like a canary right now, that nigga comment would get you strung up like a pig in a slaughterhouse." He snaps his fingers in a rapid succession to show how fast he wants the muscle to move.

As the guys pull Officer Menendez toward the crane, I notice the raw skin around his wrist oozing a little puss and I make a mental note to have the doctor check it out. Officer Menendez struggles with the guys, but is quickly overpowered.

"Mother fucking fucker! You just wait. I'ma cut cho dick off and feed your balls to the pigeons at Buckingham Fountain." He spits at Leonard and it lands smack dab in his eye. Leonard grabs him by the collar and raises his fist.

"Don't," says Reverend Pookie just before Leonard makes contact with Officer Menendez's nose.

Leonard holds him tight around his neck and threatens him through clenched teeth. Ed separates the two, and then blindfolds Officer Menendez. He hooks his wrist to the crane and pulls the end of the chain to lift him a few feet off the floor. After cutting off his t-shirt, Ed turns on the water hose and soaks Officer Menendez from head to toe.

Leonard picks up the wand and turns on the machine. Upon hearing the light buzzing, Officer Menendez jumps and moves his head from left to right as if he can see which side it would be coming from. Leonard turns the machine off. After Menendez calms down, Leonard quickly turns the wand back on and off several times just to watch Officer Menendez's response to the sound. Each time he turns it on, they bend over laughing at his reaction.

"Get on with it!" I yell.

The guys start handlin' their business after they realize that I'm watching them.

When Reverend Pookie sees I'm up here, he comes to holla' at me. "Chay Chay, my man. Didn't know you was here."

"Just checking on the progress."

"Yeah, Pig's 'bout to break any minute now. Call themselves The Star of David Officers. Can you believe that shit?" Reverend Pookie takes off that hot ass hat. "Five hundred deep in Chicago and started one in Detroit."

"Every dirty cop society has a chapter in Detroit. Pigs." I shake my head in disgust. "So what's taking this so long?"

"Well, The Star of David only give each potna half da' info, just in case only one of dem get caught. Den dere won't be enough info to work wit'. Washington ratted his half already, but his potna holding out."

I look back down at Officer Menendez screaming while Leonard looks like he's enjoying watching the wand send bolts of electricity through Officer Menendez's body.

"Did you tell him that we'd protect him and his family?"

"Yeah, but he's been brainwashed into falling fa' da' okie doke."

After about thirty minutes, Leonard looks up at us and asks, "How much longer, Boss?"

"Whatcha think?" Reverend Pookie looks at me with knowing eyes.

We look down at Leonard and Ed and say at the same time, "All nighter."

Die Trying

I believe that every single event in life
that happens is an opportunity to
choose love over fear.

—Oprah Winfrey

Jazz_____

It could simply be the lawyer in me as Asia always claims or it could actually be something. I like to think my profession and paranoia don't go hand in hand. Or it could be my hormones as Amber is so quick to point out every single day. Now, both of these theories have some validity at times. But right now, I have proof. Okay, maybe not proof, just circumstantial evidence. But many good lawyers have won cases on less.

Chase has been acting strangely lately. He's been coming in late almost *every* night for a month as well as leaving before daybreak. No breakfast in the oven waiting on me, no note saying sorry I had to leave, no call later in the day offering explanation.

Nothing. I can't remember the last time we went on our weekly date. And I know we ain't held a conversation where we put more than six sentences together this entire month.

Not to mention, he's grown a full beard and a nappy afro. It's not unbecoming; it's just......different. I think he likes his new Maxwell look. Just woke up and decided that he wanted to be Maxwell.

Chase is my best friend. We talk about everything and to be at this point where he doesn't feel comfortable enough to tell me what's going on is unnerving. Now I'm trying not to automatically think that he's cheating on me, but what else could he be doing. He could have a whole nother family or life somewhere for the amount of hours he's gone.

Then, if I walk into the room while he's on the phone, he does one of three things. He either rushes off the phone, starts whispering, or walks in the other room. Now because eavesdropping has been an effective strategy long before I got married, I want to use it. But because he's on his cell phone, I can't pick up a different receiver. And the few times that I tried to look at his call log, he'd already deleted the numbers. No incoming, outgoing, or missed calls.

This is pissing me off. I don't have anyone to talk to. Maybe I can talk to Asia's sister, India. She's still in town and she seems like she would give good advice. Nah, her head doesn't seem like it's in the right place lately.

I'm trying not to think the worse. I know Chase. We've been together forever. He adores me and would never violate our love. An affair? That's unthinkable.

But hell, what do I know? Lately, I can't think my way out of a paper bag. *Damn dumb analogy.* In my right mind, I would never say anything so dumb. Because if there is a human size paper bag, can it hold human weight? If it can, then it's not paper. And if it can't, then you wouldn't have to think because it would bust open right away.

Boy, I put way too much thought into that. I'm losing my damn mind.

What if he is messing around on me? Nah, that's not possible. But what if.....nah. I need a plan. I will figure this out or die trying.

Twirling around to seek solace in Lake Michigan is futile. The storm that has been raging for a week now is making it difficult to relax. The clouds were white at the beginning of the week, now the sky is a hodgepodge of charcoal and black with the raindrops screaming down. The Magnificent Mile has lost it bravura under the brutal attack of nature. The taxicabs are the only pulse on the streets. The thunder claps catching me off guard. I rub my stomach, feeling the instinct to comfort my baby during this tumultuous storm.

It's Not Over

Life is not a spectator sport. If you're going to
spend your whole life in the grandstand just
watching what's going on, in my opinion
you're wasting your life.

—Jackie Robinson

Chase____

November 2006

"So Chase, it's over, huh?"

"Yes Sir," I say while I pour the syrup on my French toast. I
pass him the butter dish and syrup. "Menendez took forever to
break," I say prepared to be debriefed over breakfast.

"Expected that. His father was one of the first MS-13's. The
gang put the Salvi's on the map here in Chicago. So he knows
torture."

I slice my French toast and stuff it in my mouth. *This shit is
good as hell.* Can't remember the last time I sat down and had a

meal. Ain't been able to eat nothing in weeks. So busy trying to take care of this problem that I couldn't think straight.

"Have they been relocated? Because when everything goes down, you know that it will easily be traced back to them. People are going to know that they are not dead because—"

"Yes, because when their families disappear without a trace, suspicion will rise."

"And heads will roll," I add as I pour myself a third cup of orange juice. *Damn, I didn't know I was hungry like that.*

"Well, we've taken precaution to make sure that everyone remains safe."

We take a minute to eat most of our breakfast silently. I look at his salt and pepper hair faded close to his head with a full salt and pepper beard trimmed close to his chubby face. His well-manicured hands show that he has never worked hard a day in his life.

His deep soothing voice makes me wish that he were my father. I always hate that wish. That's a dumb wish. Wishing that somebody is your daddy. Your daddy is who your daddy is and ain't nothing you can do to change that. But every time I'm with him, my *grown ass* has this adolescent ass wish.

"You've done a good service over the years, Chase."

"Thank you, Sir."

"Now, that fatherhood is about to rain down on you, it may be time to back out of the game."

I stop chewing, then begin again slowly before I swallow the food that threatens to get stuck in my throat. "That's not necessary, Sir."

"Yes, I think it is," he makes the statement sound more like an order.

"With all due respect Sir, you were a father and you never got out."

"And I wish I had."

I hold my head down, thinking about leaving the organization. Fourteen Faces was created by a group of angry flower children during the Civil Rights Movement. While the Black Panthers, SNCC, and the Mississippi Freedom Democratic Party were being demobilized, the FBI could never find its leadership, so Fourteen Faces was able to slip under the radar, becoming inactive or non-existent to the government. That's just what Fourteen Faces wanted. That gave them time to build and strengthen themselves. The sole purpose of the organization is to protect the underprivileged, uninformed, or uneducated. Those who cannot effectively protect themselves.

In the sixteen years that I've been involved, my division has brought down dirty cop organizations in nine major cities, neutralized gangs in Chicago, and put over two hundred people in state and federal government posts. From as high up as the U.S. Senate all the way down to the custodians. All to keep government honest. One member of Fourteen Faces is strategically positioned to be appointed to the cabinet of the next President of the U.S.

No I love Faces too much to walk away now.

I look him straight in the eyes. "And give up everything that you've accomplished? Faces takes derelicts, criminals, and murderers like me and train them to become citizens against corruption. You save them from a life of crime and imprisonment. Without you, I know I'd be in jail or in my grave right now. And no telling how many people I would have taken with me, in the name of......" I haven't spoken the name of my gang since being initiated into Faces and I ain't gon' start now. "No, no Sir, I don't believe that you would do anything different. Not for one minute do I believe that."

Just then, I think about Shaun's double dippin' nonsense and realize that he has absolutely no clue of what *real* double dippin' is when my cell phone rings. I take it off my hip and look at the caller id. Speak of the devil. *Shit!* I hold up the cell phone and ask, "Sir, do you mind?"

"No, no, go ahead. I need to take a bathroom break anyway."

When he is out of the room I answer the call, "Man, where the hell you at?"

"I'm at a hotel downtown." I hear music in the background and what sounds like a party going on this early in the morning.

"I told you that Asia needed you and you haven't been home yet. What the fuck is your problem, Shaun?"

"Ahhhh, C-Dog, don't lynch a brotha. I've been tied up in dealings. I'ma go see her tonight."

"Yeah, you betta'."

"No for real, I'm turning over a new leaf," Shaun says and I can sense his eyebrow twitching.

"Listen Shaun, I got something really important to tell you. I was trying to wait 'til I saw you in person, but it can't wait any longer."

"What is it, C-Dog?"

"Shaun, you got a daughter."

He laughs. "That's the big news, Dog? That's what's got cho' panties in a bunch? Well, relax, cuz it ain't mine."

"I'm serious Man."

"Not as serious as me. Wuttin' me, didn't do it. Even got documentation to prove it," he sings freestyle and I bet he's dancing too.

I dismiss his dismissal and start to explain, "Yeah, well see, the story is—"

"C-Dog, I'm fixed.

"Fixed?"

"Yeah, a vasectomy. I ain't never wanted no kids, so I got a vasectomy and didn't tell nobody. Plus, it's easier to handle my bizness when I ain't gotta worry about a million little me's running around trying to be the first to the finish line." He laughs. "I especially didn't tell Asia, cuz her clock gon' eventually tick like every other woman in the world. And where I come from time and clocks *do not* exist."

"You never told me that," I say feeling a little betrayed and upset that our sons won't grow up together.

"Yeah, about ten years ago, I was snipped and clipped, so a brotha' can't trip," he laughs again.

"Oh ten years ago. No, this happened way before that. Amber's twenty something."

"Amber?" Shaun finally stops laughing.

"Yeah, Asia put Amber up for adoption when she was sixteen."

Shaun is silent. I dare to say speechless because that has never happened in the twenty years that I've known him.

"Damnit, C-Dog, I knew something. I felt something. From

the first time I saw Amber at my birthday party, I felt a connection. It was strange too. Really strange. For her to be so beautiful, I never wanted to screw her."

Yeah, that's really strange for you cuz you'll fuck a hole in the wall. "Did you ever ask Asia about Amber? Like who is she and why is she staying at your house?"

"No. I was just happy that she had some company and wasn't hounding me about coming home. But it was weird. After Amber moved in, I wanted to come home."

Some more shit that he hadn't told me.

"When I'd come home and hear Amber and Asia in the room laughing together, I felt like I was coming home to something. I stopped bringing Asia gifts home because I felt guilty for not bring-ing Amber anything. I didn't know why. Couldn't identify it then, but now I know. I was coming home to my family. And it felt good."

"Good, well you can just go home right now and fix this."

"I don't think it's gon' be that simple. I've fucked up bad this time, C-Man."

What could be worse than what you've been doing? "Well, what you gon' do?" I ask.

"This is bad," he says more to himself than to me. "I have to close out this final thing tonight and then I'ma go home. You think you can come help me?"

"I can't keep bailing yo' ass out, Shaun!"

"This is the last time. I swear to God." I hear the music get louder and then go off.

He turned the music off? Maybe he's serious this time. "Okay, I'm in a meeting all day. I'll call you when I'm done."

"Yeah okay Dog." Shaun sounds like he's in deep thought. "And can you pick up some red roses? Asia likes them."

"Yeah, man whatever. See you tonight."

Just as I hang up the phone, he comes back from the bathroom. He sits back down in his chair and looks me straight in the eyes.

"Look Chase, just take a few years to bond as a family. Fourteen Faces will always be here, but these first years with your son only happen once."

"Sir, I'm sure Jazz will understand. I'll just tell her and—"

"NO!" he slams his fist down on the table causing plates to violently rattle and orange juice to spill. "She can never know. Nobody can know. You're an artist, no more, no less." He regains his composure and lowers his voice. "It's too dangerous."

I look at this man who I respect greatly and know that he is right. Everything he says makes sense. My food suddenly has a bitter aftertaste and is heavy on my stomach.

He sees my hesitation and adds, "At least take a short break."

"How long we talking?"

"Four, five years at the most," he says.

"Make it two, and we got a deal."

He leans back in the chair and tilts his head to the side like he often does when he is making an important call. He leans back forward, puts his hand out, and says, "Deal."

I shake his hand, but really feel an emptiness in the pit of my stomach. I'm losing a part of me and I don't know if I can survive it. I don't know if my marriage can survive it.

Messing up
a Fairytale

Once in a while, in the middle of an
ordinary life, love gives us a fairytale.

—unknown

Jazz_____

"Dad? Didn't know you were here." I wobble over to the table and interrupt him shaking hands with Chase. I kiss my daddy on the cheek.

"Morning Pumpkin. How's my girl? And how's my grandson?" He rubs my stomach.

I hold his hand on my stomach, "He's a little cranky today."

"Looks like he's ready to jump outta there any minute now." He smiles at my stomach and then at me.

"Oh contraire. I'm ready to kick him out. But he still has another month." I bend down and give Chase a kiss on the lips. "Hey Hon."

"Good Morning, Baby." He hops up and pulls my chair out for me. "Me and your dad already ate. Let me get your breakfast. You want French toast?"

"Just juice. Baby doesn't want anything heavy today."

"Plain toast?"

Hmmm, he's more attentive today. "Bagel will be fine. Or maybe I should ask him." I look down at my stomach, "Is a bagel okay with you today, Mr. Man?" And I actually wait for a response.

Chase bends down. "Daddy's boy ain't giving ya' Momma a hard time this morning are you? You gotta eat to be strong enough to be daddy and granddaddy's lil' soldier." He kisses my belly.

He walks over to the refrigerator, grabs the orange juice, a few oranges, strawberries, blueberries and my prenatal vitamins. He puts it all through the blender and then mixes it in the shaker.

"So Dad, what brings you to this side of town so early in the morning?"

"Well, I was going to surprise you and take you out to breakfast, but when I got here, Chase had that covered. He was looking like a chef in there, so I decided, I think I wanna eat here instead of at Edna's. So we just ate breakfast and he updated me about everything that has been going on in my absence. You know, the late night cravings, baby room decorations, ultrasounds, and stuff. He couldn't stop talking about how excited he is about his son."

I look over at Chase who's smiling as he spreads the strawberry jam on my bagel. He glances over at me and I know at that moment that he would never cheat on me. *God, I love that man.*

He brings the juice and bagel and sits it down in front of me. "Would you like anything else, Madame?" he asks in his exaggerated British accent.

Yeah, I want something, but I can't say it in front of my daddy.
"No thanks Hon, this is quite enough." I say and then smile at my very first love and ask, "So Daddy, how long are you home for?"

"Well Pumpkin, actually, I'm thinking about retiring."

Shock grabs me by the throat and I choke on the bagel that I had just attempted to swallow. Chase jumps up and pats me on the back until the piece comes up.

My whole life has been laced with memories of my dad being in and out of the country for extended periods of time. Making it home the day before a major holiday or just in time for me or Lonnie's birthday party. There was never a time when he was easily accessible. Always out of the country, locked in his library, or sleeping from working long hours. Mixed emotions pop up all over me when the realization hits home.

"Well, if that's the response I'ma get every time I tell somebody, I may just work until I croak."

"No, no, Daddy. I'm really happy. I'm just....I just...It's just...."

"I know. I heard it all from your mother when I told her. I decided that I'm getting too old to keep working this hard. It's time to pass the buck on to the young fellows." He and Chase look at each other like they're in the same line of work.

"Yeah, you may wanna toss the baton to the sturdy stallions so we can show you old cats how it's done." Chase does his one-handed Tarzan chest bang and laughs.

"Oh, you think you young bucks can teach me something, huh? I had traveled around the world seventy-five times before you was even out of diapers."

Chase laughs. "I don't know how you did that. I heard it took you and your buddy, Columbus, a whole six years to find the Americas."

The doorbell rings and I'm happy to get out of there because the two of them can play the dozens for hours. I open the door and Amber is standing there with a stack of file folders.

Confusion must have been written across my face because she says, "Of course you don't remember, but can you at least fake it? Everyone doesn't have to know that you have pregnancy brain." Then she bends down and talks to my stomach. "And don't let her blame this on you, Sweetie. She had pregnancy brain long before she got pregnant. See, right now she's trying to remember my name." Amber laughs.

"Ha, ha. I think I hear Apollo calling you to the stage." I close the door as she sits the folders on the cocktail table. "And as a matter of fact, I do remember that we had a uh....that uh... thing to do this morning," I lie while searching my brain for the information.

"Uhn huh? And what thing would that be exactly?"

"You know. That thing we talked about yesterday. About, you know."

"Yeah, I know. The problem is that you, Missy, do not know. Now you see that hanging by your front door with the post it note on it?" Amber points to the tack board on my wall that is labeled "My Memory Board."

I look over at the board with about six post-it notes on it. "Yeah."

"You see the red one."

"Yeah there's one red, three yellows and two greens."

"Well, anytime you have a red one, that mean that you have a deadline that falls on a Monday and you asked me to bring the files to you because you want to stop going into the office on the weekends. This file needs to be closed out on Monday, so you called me last night because you *forgot them* at the office and needed me to be here, and this is a quote, 'before noon because I really, really need to get this done.' Remember?" She asks and shakes her head at me. "Does any of this sound familiar?"

I stare blankly at her. I can't remember two plus two lately.

"Now I'm here at 11:45 and you looking at me like I'm the alien. I tell you, pregnant people."

She smiles and passes me the files. I look through them thinking how happy I am to see Amber in good spirits. She hasn't been the same since Asia tried to kill herself. Now that Asia has accepted her as her daughter and officially let her move into the condo, she is a totally different person and she seems to be getting back to her old self. Asia is even planning some type of debutante, coming out party. I told her that Amber was too old for that, but whatever. If planning a party will keep her from hanging herself, then so be it.

It only takes a couple of minutes for me to look through the files. I can still hear my daddy and Chase in there going at it. Sounds like they may have moved on to "Yo' Momma" jokes.

Amber says in a far distant voice, "Jazz, who is that in there with Chase? That voice sounds very familiar."

"Oh, come in here. We've been sitting here all this time. What was I thinking? Now this is a 'duh' moment. Come, come, I want you to meet someone." I brace myself with my hands behind me and push up off the sofa.

For a moment Amber hesitates.

"Come on, I promise he doesn't bite." I grab her hand and lead her into the kitchen.

"Daddy, I want you to meet my assistant, Amber." My daddy turns around with his mouth open, but nothing comes out.

"Do you two know each other?" I ask in the awkward moment.

"No," they both say a little too quickly.

Then, before even acknowledging Amber, he asks, "What happened to Rebecca?"

"Well, she decided to study for the Bar again, thanks to Amber."

"Well, Amber, it's nice to meet you." Daddy extends his hand.

"Likewise."

We stand there for another awkward moment before Chase says, "You didn't tell him the most exciting news of all. Amber is Asia and Shaun's teenage love child that she put up for adoption without telling him. Amber searched until she found her real mother. And then it's some fairytale ending after that."

"You don't say?" my father smiles.

Amber shrugs, "Well everything, but the fairytale part. If you know anything about my mother, you know she can mess up a fairytale at any given moment."

"Ditto to that," I say.

"Well, nice meeting you Mr....um?"

"Hamilton. Mr. Hamilton," my dad extends his hand again.

Amber and I go back to the living room to grab our work and take it into the office. We are locked in that office for a few hours before my dad comes in to say goodbye.

"I'ma be on my way, Pumpkin."

"Leaving already?"

"I have a lot of work to do before I retire," he kneels down, puts his mouth on my stomach, and whispers to the baby for a few seconds. The baby kicks twice. My daddy backs away and asks, "Oh, so you do understand?" And the two of us laugh.

He stands and turns to Amber. "You keep up the good work, Amber. You're definitely in good company. Let me give you my card, so that if you ever need anything you can reach me." He pulls his wallet out of his pocket and searches for a business card. "Oh, I don't have any in my wallet. I think I have a few extra ones in my car. Do you mind walking out with me and I'll give you one?"

"No Sir, I mean Mr. Hamilton, I don't mind at all," is what her mouth says, but Amber's eyes tell another story.

The look of fear is there again. I think she's scared of my father for some reason. *Okay, Jazz, you know your pregnancy brain has been off lately so give it a rest.*

When Amber comes back in, she seems a little withdrawn, but she says it's because she's tired. So we finish up within an hour, and she decides to take a nap on the lounge chair in the office before she heads home.

I walk upstairs to check on Chase. Not only is he dressing to go, but he's cut his hair and shaved his full beard back into a goatee. He looks like the man that I know and love, but I still feel a little uneasy. Like the distance that has grown between us over the past month is about to widen.

"Going somewhere?" I ask trying to take the accusatory tone out of my voice. Didn't work.

"Um, gotta meet with um....somebody to close out some important stuff."

Vague. "Oh." I sit on the bed and watch him pick out his

clothes. "How long you think you gon' be gone?"

"Hard to say, two maybe three hours. I'm hoping it won't take very long, but you know how these things go."

Didn't even make our six sentence quota this time. I don't think he's looked at me once since I've been in the room. I want to scream and yell for him not to leave, but I can't. I have no reason to be suspicious of him or insecure. *Hormones. Just the hormones.*

We make small talk for about a half hour with me asking questions and him answering simply yes or no until his cell phone rings. And, of course, he does one of those three things—walks in another room. Well, this time, I decide to listen at the door.

"Which hotel?" Chase is asking, which isn't all that alarming because he meets out of town clients at their hotels all the time. His second question and the familiar tone with which he addresses the caller, however, send off the alarm bells. "The Ritz Carlton in the Water Tower? Are you crazy? Do they rent by the hour because I know that has to be an arm and a leg?"

I put my hand over my mouth to stifle a whimper and anger dries the tears that threatened to fall. I'm too pissed to cry.

"Jasmine, I'm gone," he calls sounding like he's already at the door and angry about how much money he has to spend on his booty call. And did he just call me Jasmine? He never calls me Jasmine. It's always Jazz or Jazzy or Babe or something endearing. Never Jasmine.

"I'm taking your car," he yells and slams the door.

Did somebody just mess up my fairytale?

Let's Roll

When a friend is in trouble, don't annoy him
by asking if there is anything you can do.
Think up something appropriate and do it.

—Edgar Watson Howe

Amber_____

When I wake up in Jazz's office, everything comes back to me. Meeting her father, Mr. Hamilton. And that voice. The Voice. The voice of the man who has been giving me my orders for almost 7 years now. Seeing the man behind the voice and fearing what the implication of seeing this enigmatic mystery man would bring. When walking to the car with him, the only comfort I have is in knowing that the organization doesn't do random killings.

All of the missions that I did were for the greater good of society. I did my research on every person who I had to take out, and they were demons. Participating in mass murders on a large scale to confiscate land in third world countries or funding child sex rings with girls and boys who hadn't made it to double digit ages. Or it could be something not so malicious, but deadly nonetheless like dumping toxins into a city's water supply and causing cancers or hundreds of deaths and beating the class action suit because you paid off the Prosecutor. Fourteen Faces is a cross between a modern day Robin Hood and a militia vigilante.

At his car, he assured me that I had nothing to worry about and that no harm would come to me or Karob. And although, we both have been officially released of our debt to his organization, Karob had decided to stay on and become a member of Fourteen Faces. He said that they seldom used women and that I had been a first, but if I needed anything, just call. With that, he gave me his card and left. Leaving me to think about the first time I heard that voice.

I had been staying in that Motel 6 for a month after I killed my adopted father for being my pimp when I woke up one morning with a woman sitting at the foot of my bed. She was not threatening or aggressive and her serene voice gave me comfort that I had never felt in my life.

"We know you killed your father," the woman says.

I didn't answer because I wasn't presented with a question.

"We also know that you are underage and should be in foster care."

Again, I just stared at her, feeling like this was all part of some bigger plan. And knowing that if I were going to jail or something, they would have woke me up. There's no such thing as a "last sleep" like when you get a "last meal."

Not once did I feel anxious, uneasy, or hesitant. I knew that whatever she asked me to do could never be any worse than what my adopted father had forced me to do.

I never knew her name, but she told me that I'd be coming with her. She took me to set up a bank account with an international chain and not a local bank. Access to my money worldwide is always a plus, she explained. She also found a management company to rent out the house that I never knew I owned. The management company would deal with the renter and any repairs for a small fee. The rest of the money would be deposited into an escrow account. She made sure that my father's pension and insurance payout were also deposited into one of my three bank accounts before we left the city. And all of this was done on a Sunday when everything was supposed to be closed. She was a handler.

When we boarded that plane going to Chicago, I was a little apprehensive. Although I never had a happy day after my adopted mother died, that was still all the life I knew. And to get up and leave without a single word to anyone? Chicago could've been Bangladesh for all I knew at sixteen. But I put on a good front.

Just as the plane touched down in Chicago, she said, "From now on, you'll be known as Amber. Amber Cherrington."

Amber Cherrington? That's sophisticated.

Fourteen Faces has for years hand-picked people who fit a profile constructed by their organization. One part of the selection profile was that the participants be between the ages of sixteen and nineteen. These teenagers had to have committed a planned, calculated murder. The final requirement is that we would never be missed if we disappeared.

Ten of us, all teenagers, sat in that room listening to the soothing voice of Mr. Hamilton explain what our lives would be like until we became of age. A gruesome regiment. I felt like I was in the military. Up by five in the morning for conditioning and skills training.

We were taught extraordinary skills like sword fighting, use of a bow and arrow, throwing a javelin, and how to breathe underwater for an extended period of time. Outside of breathing underwater, I've only had to use one of those skills.

All of that was learned before we were sent to Thailand to study Muay Thai, one of the deadliest forms of martial arts the world has ever known. We were sent there every summer for two and a half months. Trained for eight to ten hours a day.

School was never neglected. We had three subjects only: math because it's universal, international politics, and chemistry. This is all that was required to complete the jobs that they had in store for us. If we wanted to read Moby Dick or Julius Caesar, we had to do it on our own time. And since we didn't have much time, that didn't happen. Writing was not part of the curriculum, so we learned to write from whatever textbook we had.

We all saw psychiatrists seven days a week. There were three different types of sessions. One psychiatrist focused on our family life and the social environment in which we were raised. That was my Dr. Pleasant. She was a quack. The second psychiatrist tracked our emotional health and identified any new emotional or psychological problems that may be developing due to the adjustment to a lifestyle that is so intense. Another quack. The last psychiatrist was also a metaphysician who taught us how to meditate and control our energy, chakras, and vibrations. I enjoyed that the most. I like being in control.

I pick up a picture of Jazz as a young girl sitting on her father's lap. *Some people are so lucky. I have two loser daddies. How the hell does that happen?*

I hear something crash on the floor in the kitchen. I go in there to find Jazz franticly searching for something.

"What's the matter?"

She jumps, "Oh my God. I forgot you were here. You scared me half to death." She turns back around and continues to look.

"Whatcha looking for?" I ask trying to sound casual, although she's looking kinda crazy.

"Keys, I need Chase's keys. He took my car and I need to make a run."

"I can take you wherever you need to go. You don't look like you're in any condition to be driving."

"No Amber, you can't go. If Asia knew I took her daughter where I'm going, she'd never forgive me."

I pick up Shaun's car keys that are sitting on the kitchen table in plain sight and say, "Well, since I have the only two sets of car keys in the house, I suggest you get over your guilt. And quickly."

Jazz looks at me like she thought about thinking twice, but then quickly says, "Let's roll then."

On the way to the Ritz Carlton, Jazz tells me about Chase being out late at night and leaving early in the morning and acting strangely. About him being all secretive and deleting all of his calls. She had given him the benefit of the doubt until she eaves-dropped on his conversation. Now, she is convinced that he was messing around. I wasn't convinced yet.

When we pull up to the Ritz, we see Chase at the valet and he buys the last dozen of roses from a guy standing outside the hotel. Jazz begins to cry at this point.

Butcher
Knife Therapy

Rain beats a leopard's skin, but
it doesn't wash off the spots.

—Ashanti Proverb

Asia____

*O*da walks in and hands me an envelope. She hasn't been able to look me in the eyes since I've returned from the hospital. I can't tell if she pities me, is angry with me, or just doesn't like me. It's not a secret that Shaun is the only reason why she's lasted this long. Yeah, I'll give her two weeks pay in the morning and relieve her of her duties.

I open the envelope and inside is a keycard and a note that says, *Want to see what your husband's doing tonight?* And I realized that I do have a score to settle with Shaun.

I go into the bathroom to clean my wrist and change the gauze. There is not a single sign that just two weeks ago, I had tried to kill myself in this very bathroom. Amber had gone through great lengths to make sure of that. Before I came home, the mirror had been replaced, as well as the floor tile that had been stained by my blood. There was, evidently, a chip on the countertop from when the soap dispenser fell on it. She replaced that with one of the two marble tops that we had debated over. Of course she chose her preference. It looks good.

I look over to the chaise that Amber has slept on every night since I've come home from the hospital. Well, most mornings when I wake up, she's in the bed with me. I smile thinking about how happy she makes me. Is this what they mean by unconditional love? Children love their parents unconditionally. Or is it the other way around? I can't believe that I missed out on so much of my daughter's life. And every time I ask about her adoptive parents, she only says that they both died and shuts down. She's allowed one secret. I had mine.

When I came back from visiting Dartmouth my sophomore year of high school, I was pregnant with Shaun's baby. Since I was young and inexperienced with no morning sickness or weight gain, I didn't know I was pregnant until I was six months. I wasn't alarmed that I didn't have a menstrual. My menstrual wasn't regular anyway at that age and honestly, I was happy it was gone. Well, when I got a little pooch in my stomach I took a pregnancy test. After I went for a physical and prenatal vitamins, I contacted an adoption agency in Louisiana. The only thing that I asked of them was that they arrange to induce labor on a certain weekend so that I could get away without my parents knowing.

Now look where I am. On my way to the Ritz Carlton, to confront my husband and his hoe. I stop at the gun shop to purchase a pearl-handled pistol. I've always wanted one of those. I walk up to the counter and ask the white guy who is reading the Chicago Sun-Times, "Do you have any pearl handles?"

He looks down at my wrist and says, "We all outta pearls," and goes back to reading his paper.

"Well, I guess any little old gun will do."

He glances up from his newspaper like I am bothering him and looks me down and back up from my Dodgers baseball cap to my shades, trench coat, and Gucci tennis shoes. He looks back at the gauze around my wrist and says, "I would have to do a background check and that'll take a couple weeks. Here, fill this out." He slides me the background check form.

So on to Plan B. I was hoping it didn't come to this because I really wasn't trying to break a nail, not to mention that I am wearing my favorite Burberry coat and scarf. But what's a girl to do? So, I stop at a Kmart and pick up a butcher knife. Butcher knives have solved many domestic disputes over the centuries. If a butcher knife didn't change a man, nothing could.

When a Woman's Fed Up

Never once did she say "Where have
you been?" She said "Are you hungry?
Are you hungry, Honey? Did you eat?"

—The Persuaders

*J*azz's life is crashing down around her as her heart is being ripped from her chest. Amber looks out of the window at Chase, shakes her head and wonders how her asshole radar could have been so off. *My instincts are always right,* Amber laments at her failure.

Jazz reaches up and grabs Chase's gun that he keeps tucked in his sun visor and quickly puts it in her purse. *I can kill his ass,* Jazz thinks. Amber turns around as Jazz zips up her purse.

"You know, you don't have to do this. What's the point of seeing it?" Amber asks, hoping to talk some sense into Jazz, but Jazz steps out of the car.

Inside the hotel, people are moving at a hurried pace. Even the people standing still look like they're moving fast. Like Chase. Although he's at the registration desk, he looks like he's jogging in place or something. His demeanor is screaming, 'Hurry the hell up.'

"A friend left a key for me. Penthouse Suite Number Four," Chase says clenching his molars down hard while cursing out Shaun in his head for having him out when he'd rather be at home rubbing Jazz's feet. *This is the last fucking time I'm bailing his ass out. He needs to grow the fuck up.*

"The fucking penthouse? What stupid ass gets a penthouse for a booty call?" Jazz asks the rhetorical question as the realization of Chase's infidelity sinks in and kicks her in the gut. *Or was that the baby,* she wonders.

"You'd be surprised," Amber says, not really wanting to be involved, but knowing that she couldn't leave Jazz alone in her hysteria. She wouldn't be able to explain that decision to her mother or Mr. Hamilton, who she knew she'd be seeing more often when he retires.

"All the late nights when he claimed his cell phone was not getting reception. And I fell for that bullshit."

"Why don't you just talk to him tonight?" Amber suggests and tries to think whether she's ever heard Jazz curse.

Jazz either ignores her or is in her own world right now, "There's no way we're getting up to the penthouse," Jazz watches Chase get on the elevator labeled Penthouse Levels Only.

Amber sighs when she sees Jazz is not budging. "I sorta got a way," Amber reluctantly admits because she knows that if the roles were reversed, she would want to eliminate the "wuttin me" bailout. And cut off a dick if necessary. *I'm not above Lorena Bobbitt,* Amber thinks.

Upstairs, Chase walks into the Penthouse and hears *So Amazing* by Luther coming from the bedroom. *So he's turned the music back on. That didn't last long. Let me piss before I deal with him.* Chase goes into the bathroom and tries to figure out if it's worth it. *Probably not. I've been doing this shit for years and he still hasn't changed.*

As he listens to Luther sing, "Truly it's amazing, amazing. Love's brought us together, together. I would leave you never and.....," he decides that he's going back home to Jazz after he uses the bathroom.

He has a wife and a son on the way to worry about now. "Lil' Chase." He shakes his head. "C-Man, nah." He shakes his head again. "Lil' Chay Chay." *Oh, hell naw.* "Junior," he says and smiles. "Yeah, Junior." He's got Junior to worry about now, so he can't be caught up in Shaun's mess. Chase decides that Shaun is on his own with this one and that he's about to leave the hotel room and go home to his wife

In the lobby while walking up to the elevator, Amber discreetly presses a button on her watch which stalls the cameras in the hotel long enough for them to get to the Penthouse, which has no cameras. Once on the elevator, she pulls a key card out of her wallet and sticks it in the slot to be given access to the private suites.

Jazz doesn't ask any questions. Right now, she doesn't care. Not to mention that her baby is curling up really tightly causing her stomach to cramp. She has always known that Amber is resourceful, but to what extent is a mystery. Jazz makes a mental note to ask Amber about it when they leave. Her baby balls up tighter. She flinches.

While Jazz and Amber are riding up to the Penthouse, Asia walks into the hotel. Although it is pitch-black and raining outside, she has on dark Bvlgari shades and a long trench coat. In her attempt to not be noticed or recognized, she inadvertently becomes noticeably unrecognizable.

Asia wants to use the restroom before she goes up to the penthouse. She takes her time to see if maybe she would change her mind. She starts remembering all the wonderful times that she and Shaun have had. She looks in the mirror and says, "Maybe we can give it another shot. Work it out," but her better half asks, *Bitch are you crazy?*

Meanwhile, Jazz and Amber approach the door with nothing on it but the word "Four." Amber turns to Jazz who looks as if she's not all there, and before she could speak, Jazz says, "Just open the door, Amber."

Amber hesitates before she puts the key card in the door. Inside the penthouse, all is quiet except for the soothing sound of Luther singing, *Here and Now.*

That's our wedding song. Jazz's heart sinks.

Jazz's baby begins doing his protest march again. She grabs her stomach and bends over.

"You okay?"

"Baby has lost his damn mind too." And with that statement, the baby curls up into a tight ball again, causing her to cramp even harder than she had earlier. She jerks, but ignores the pain temporarily and walks towards the music. Amber walks behind her.

"Amber wait here. I need to do this by myself." Amber takes a seat on the sofa.

Jazz slowly walks toward the door with Luther professing, "Your love is all I need. Ooh ooh, yeah, yeah, yeah, yeah, yeah, yeah, yeah." She pushes the door open just as the song is ending and Amber can hear the moans of satisfaction from her position on the sofa.

The curtains are drawn making it impossible for Jazz to see anything. The only light in the room is generating from two Victoria's Secret candles that are making the room smell of mangoes or strawberries or both. She can't tell. But there's nothing wrong with her hearing, so when she hears the soft whispers of "I love you. I love you. I love you," she loses it.

She walks all the way up to the bed, pulls the gun out of her purse, and starts blindly shooting while mumbling to herself, "You fucking motherfucker you." The trigger, as well as her baby, seems to be pulling against her. Her baby kicks her hard three, four, then five times in protest, but it's too late.

Chase runs out of the bathroom when he hears shots ring out and sees Amber jumping up off the sofa.

"Amber?" His heart drops into his stomach before it leaps back up into his throat causing him to hyperventilate.

"Oh no, Jazz, no!" Chase runs to the bedroom with Amber right on his heels. "Jazz!" He turns on the light, grabs Jazz, spinning her around and catching her off guard.

"Chase?" The gun fires again. Time stops for the two of them, literally. Both wish that they were at home snuggling under the cover watching *Martin*. Both wish they were eating Chase's homemade rocky road ice cream that they've named, "Da' Bomb." Both wish that they had properly said goodbye with their habitual salutatory kiss and I love you. Both wish and wish and wish.

Chase staggers back slowly. A bullet to the chest.

"Chase?" Jazz drops the gun and reaches out to grab Chase's hand as he begins to sway. Their fingertips barely touch.

"Chase?" More tears flow blurring her vision.

Chase tries to say something. He wants to say, "I love you, Jazzy," but the pain has muted his voice. His mouth moves, just like the first time that they met, but no sound is coming out.

Chase and Jazz look into each other's sorrowful, pain-stricken eyes. Both hurting physically and emotionally.

"Chase." Jazz faints. Chase gathers enough strength to catch her before they hit the floor. Her head lands on his chest, the same spot it is every night, only now she's lying in his blood.

"Oh shit!" Amber rushes to the phone on the nightstand by the bed and dials zero.

Amber sees Shaun in the bed with a bullet to the head and the woman with him has suffered the same fate. "India?" Amber knew that the tension between Shaun and India was way too strong, but she never suspected that India would sleep with her sister's husband.

She looks into the lifeless eyes of her father. A father who she never got to know, never got to talk to, never got to hug. Those are her onyx eyes. She reaches over and closes them.

"Thank you for calling the—"

"Three people have been shot in Penthouse Four. We need an ambulance."

"I'll call 911," the operator says in a voice without inflection as if she regularly gets these type of calls.

Just then, someone else walks in. "Sweeties, I'm back. Whip cream and caramel at your service."

Must be the trois of this ménage a trois, Amber thinks.

Amber rushes behind the door. When the trois walks into the room, Amber steps from behind the door, grabs her behind both ears, and targets her thumbs on the woman's pressure points before the trois passes out. Amber looks down at the woman on the floor and has to refrain from kicking her. It's Layla, Jason's fiancée. *Can't trust nobody these days.*

"Oh, what the hell? I never liked you anyway." Amber kicks Layla. Amber's calm as she surveys the scene. She has never been part of the clean up crew, but she was trained. She moves fast as lightening as she estimates that she only has about 90 seconds before the police arrive.

She picks up Jazz's gun and slips it inside her coat pocket. Then she takes a vial and a small cloth from her purse, pours the compound on the piece of cloth, and cleans Jazz's fingertips. She then reaches in her purse and takes out the pistol that she never leaves home without and puts it in Layla's hand. She grabs the vase off the table and breaks it on the floor behind Layla.

Yeah Layla, you gon' have to take the fall for this one. Shouldn't have had yo' skank ass here no way.

Now she rushes to attend to Chase. She runs to the bathroom for towels and, after moving Jazz off his chest, she is applying pressure to Chase's wound when the police rush in.

Amber has accounted for everything. No gunpowder on Jazz's

fingertips. She'll swap out Jazz's clothes at the hospital, which surely has evidence on them. The female shooter is knocked unconscious with the gun still in her hand. She knew that forensics would easily lose the gun anyway. It will be an open and shut case even without the original weapon. Yes, she has accounted for everything.

What she hadn't planned for was Jazz waking up as the police are entering the suite, still hysterical and screaming, "Oh Chase! I'm sorry Chase. I didn't mean to—" Amber grabs Jazz and puts her to sleep the same way she had done Layla.

Asia steps off the elevator to find the floor swarming with Chicago Police Officers. They are all going in and out of Penthouse Four. She sees bulbs flashing and she walks in and passes several officers who don't even notice her. Although it is extremely loud in the penthouse, all sound is muted when she steps into the bedroom.

Asia first sees Jazz lying on the floor with blood coming from her head and Chase being lifted onto a dolly with blood coming from his torso. *Oh my God!*

Then, she looks over to the bed where the crime scene investigator is taking pictures. The view of the bed is blocked but when the investigator moves, she sees Shaun and India's lifeless bodies lying in the bed, both with bullet holes to the head. Asia doesn't know who to mourn first.

"No," she whispers and shakes her head in disbelief. *This can't be happening.* "Agggghhhhh! Noooo!" she screams.

"Who the hell is this lady? Get her outta here goddamnit!" an officer yells.

"Oh God, no!" Asia screams. "No, no, no!"

Amber looks up from where she is being questioned and rushes over to Asia and hugs her, "Mommie, I'm sorry." She leads her out the suite. "Mommie, I'm sorry. I'm sorry." Asia buries her face on Amber's shoulder and cries.

Amber calls Mr. Hamilton to have him arrange for someone to pick up Asia and to get the other processes rolling to clean this mess up.

While Amber stays around for questioning and to lay the ground work for Layla's arrest, Jazz is in the ambulance telling one of the paramedics, "I didn't mean to kill them. I'm sorry. I didn't mean to."

She tells the nurses in the emergency room, the doctors who treat her, and the police officers who are there to arrest her after she gives birth to Chase Amanuel Livingston, Jr.

Epilogue

Asia____

My best friend is accused of killing my first love. The man who I gave my virginity to. The father of my only child. My lying, cheating, no good husband. *I should probably feel a little sad, huh?*

Well, actually, I am a little upset. I wish that Jazz didn't have to spend a year in prison while on trial for a crime that she didn't commit. And I wish that India wasn't brain damaged so that I can give her a piece of my mind. It's no fun insulting a forty-year old with the mental capacity of a two-year old. And I'm *really, really* pissed off that I didn't cut off Shaun's dick with that butcher knife. Talk about icing on the cake.

I look up to the front where Jazz is seated. She's lost *soooo* much weight. Mainly from being depressed because she's not really living the prison life. Somehow, her father arranged for her to live in the Warden's quarters. She's never seen a day of general population. We get to visit her as often as we like for as long as we like. We try to cheer her up. But the truth of the matter is, she misses Chase.

Baby Chase that is. Her husband, Chase, is confined to a wheelchair. Seeing Chase debilitated, saddens me as well. The bullet damaged his spinal cord and part of it is still lodged there. The doctors will attempt to remove the bullet fracture, then he'll begin therapy. The doctors are confidant that Chase will make a full recovery, but he put off his operation to be with Jazz. Chase lives in the prison with her and only leaves for his doctor's appointments and to see the baby. However, Jazz hasn't seen Baby Chase since she delivered him in the hospital. She refuses to let us bring him to her. Not wanting him to see his mother as a prisoner. So Jazz's parents are taking care of him.

The jury has been sequestered for three months and in deliberation for four days. The District Attorney's key witness, Layla, said that she and India had been messing around with Shaun for a couple of years and that India had fallen in love with him and was trying to convince him to leave me. Well, this was a lost case for the D.A. when Layla mysteriously escaped from protective custody and fled the country, practically proving her guilt. Not to mention, that the state had no murder weapon.

What type of morons loses the evidence on such a high profile case?

So, all they had was a forced, illegally acquired, inadmissible confession of a woman in early labor who thought she had just seen her husband murdered by some crazed woman who they let escape.

Yes, Jazz was simply traumatized and delusional.

When the jury told the judge that they were hung and unable to agree, he sent them back. Now they've made their decision. I rush up front where Amber is already seated. We did not miss a day to show our support for Jazzy.

A common criminal? I think not.

"Has the jury reached a verdict?"

"Yes, your honor," the foreman stands up.

"How say you?"

"We the jury find the defendant, Jasmine Livingston, on the charge of Murder in the 1st Degree, Not Guilty."

This is the first sign of life that Jazz has shown the entire trial. She covers her face and cries. We all walk over and hug her.

When Amber reaches her, Jazz and Amber lock eyes for a long time before Jazz mouths something to Amber. It seems like she says, "Lifesaver," but that doesn't make sense. I've never been that great at lip reading.

"Let's go. Let's get outta here. I need to see my baby." Jazz takes the handle of Chase's wheelchair and pushes him out the courthouse.

Amber leads the way. If she thought she was the Queen of Sheba before, she must now believe she's Isis. She walks like all the world is at her fingertips. The great puppeteer.

My sugar-sweet baby.